LOVE & MURDER

A VIOLET CARLYLE HISTORICAL MYSTERY

BETH BYERS

AUTHOR'S NOTE

The events of Valentine's evening and the jewel thief referenced in the first chapter are available in Mystery on Valentine's Day co-written with the fabulous Lee Strauss.

If you'd like to read it for free through Kindle Unlimited or purchase your own copy, click here.

CHAPTER 1

"*L*et's just go home," Jack suggested as they left the Savoy. Once the ruckus of stolen jewelry had passed, they'd enjoyed an excellent dinner, but they had intended to go to one of their favorite dancing clubs. Or at least, Violet had intended for them to do so. She lifted her brow at him as their car approached.

"Really?" Violet asked.

Jack's eyes glinted in a way that told Violet he was up to something. It could just be that it was Valentine's evening, but she thought it might be something else. He tugged her after him towards their auto where Hargreaves had driven them out for the evening. She winked at their butler and sometime-driver and leaned forward to tell him of the stolen jewelry and meeting Ginger Gold and her husband, noting that Hargreaves hadn't asked where they were going. He had, instead, immediately turned the auto home.

Yes, Violet thought, Jack was up to something and Hargreaves was in on it. Hargreaves listened to her tale, weaving their auto through the dark London streets. He asked questions until Vi finally revealed who the thief had been.

"No!" he said as she described the final capture of the thieves.

Violet leaned back, mischief filling her expression. "You know—Hargreaves, you need a lady."

"Maybe he has one," Jack said. "Ignore her, Hargreaves. Follow your own course."

Violet elbowed Jack for interrupting her teasing. "Then why did he volunteer to look after us tonight rather than spoiling her? He needs to *find* a lady. We have other fellows who could have driven us and our Hargreaves should have been the last of those who was working."

Jack shook his head and told Hargreaves, "Don't mind her, my friend."

Hargreaves shifted and then said, "Jimmy is proposing this evening. Flowers, champagne, all the trimmings. I am working so young Jimmy can sweep his beloved off her feet."

Violet gasped and then eyed Jack. "So he's not going with some random proposal on the seashore?"

Jack groaned as Hargreaves laughed, but he tugged her under his arm. "I think you cried when I randomly proposed on the seashore."

"I'm sure I didn't," Violet lied as Jack pressed a kiss to her temple and then another to the palm of her hand.

Jack grunted, not bothering to counter her lies.

"But if you did have a lady," Violet said seriously to Hargreaves. "She'd be welcome in our home."

Hargreaves had a tinge of a blush on his cheeks as he stopped the auto outside of their home. "I appreciate that, Mrs. Vi," he said as he handed her out of the car. Jack followed, tugging her up the steps with him. As one of the maids opened the front door, her gaze glittering with sheer excitement, Violet turned to Jack and waited. Her expression made it clear that she knew something was up.

"My lady," Molly said, as she took Violet's coat. "A present arrived."

Violet turned to the parlor where the maid indicated and her jaw dropped as she saw a good dozen bouquets of roses and lilies. She walked into the flower wonderland, letting her fingers trail over the flowers, and then she turned back to Jack.

His gaze was narrowed, hands on his hips, and his jaw flexing. He was a large man with broad shoulders. In her mind, she'd thought of him often as a mountain of a man, and at the moment, her mountain seemed a little volcanic.

"Jack?" Her voice was low and soft. "What's wrong?"

"Who are they from?"

"What?" she asked, frowning. "They're not from you?"

He shook his head. He rubbed his hand over the back of his neck, and she knew it was to hide his fury. He wasn't worried that she was cuckolding him. She was sure of that.

She couldn't help but skip her mind through the possibilities. For a gift of this amount? She could only imagine Jack, her twin, or her father. But her twin had sent her a signed set of Edgar Rice Burroughs books and a painting he'd had someone make of her favorites, Tarzan and Jane. Her father rarely thought of remarking on any holiday, but he *had*, actually, sent her a gift. She'd received quite a lovely bouquet of flowers and chocolates just that morning.

"I have no idea." Violet examined the flowers with far less delight as she looked for the card. She found it in the final bouquet. She opened the envelope with Jack leaning over her shoulder. "Who would send me this but you?"

The answer was not what she expected:

> With utter devotion.
> Yours—

"What does that mean?" Jack asked. "Devotion? Why is some bloke sending you flowers? Why is some *man*—" He said 'man' like it was an insult, "—sending you something romantic on *Valentine's Day?*"

"Why didn't he sign it?" Violet demanded. "Who sent this?" Violet gestured to the flowers behind them. "They all mean varying expressions of love if you consider the language of flowers. Some—" She didn't finish when she saw the look on his face, but some meant passionate love. Given that they were *all* various meanings of love, but none that meant friendship or platonic love, she didn't think it was a mistake. It wasn't just a florist assuming. This was a message, and it made her shudder.

Jack tucked her close to him as Molly tremulously spoke up. "I—"

Jack and Vi turned to the maid and found Hargreaves tugging her from the parlor. Jack pulled Violet even closer, his hand spread over her back as if he were protecting her from something unseen. The maid whispered to Hargreaves, but he didn't stop removing her from the parlor. Jack cursed. "Hargreaves, find out if we know where they came from, even if you have to visit all the different flower shops in London."

It was a momentous task but Hargreaves didn't flinch.

"If you find the place, bribe them to find out who ordered the flowers. Whatever it costs—"

"Jack..." Violet started, hoping to calm him down. He was

already stiff and his fingers were curled into her back as if he couldn't hold her tight enough. "This doesn't have to be something nefarious."

"Violet," he countered. His tone was low and furious, but it wasn't directed at her. "This isn't jealousy, it's worry. The hair is standing up on the back of my neck."

"But why? What harm are flowers?"

"You shuddered when you realized what this was." He spoke softly—almost too gently. "Why?"

She frowned and then pulled away from him to pace among the flowers. Two bouquets on the fireplace mantel, three on the small table behind the Chesterfield, one on either table near the chairs. She nibbled her thumb and then found herself twirling her wedding ring around her finger. Finally she said, "I can't imagine who might have sent them. We have only been in London since the new year. Is it someone we've known forever? Is it some new person? We haven't been associating with new people regularly. Why would someone we've known for a while proclaim their feelings now?"

He nodded, and she realized that his worries matched her own. Something wasn't right with this. Hargreaves entered the parlor again and said something low to Jack.

"What I had planned is ready, if you'd like?" His hand was held out to her and she realized all sense of romance and holiday had fled. What she wanted was to curl up with him, near a fire, with a book. It was so much easier to ignore what was bothering her with a good book to read.

Violet took his hand and noted his gaze turning towards the table where the three bouquets were.

There was a small gift, wrapped in white paper, that she hadn't noticed amid the shock of all the flowers. She knew that Jack wanted her to ignore it, but she let go of his hand to tear open the paper and open the box.

It was a ring with a large emerald cut ruby surrounded by small diamonds, fine enough to serve as an engagement ring. She knew enough about jewelry to feel certain that its value rivaled the value of her actual engagement ring. Violet shoved the ring back as though it were a poisonous snake. It wasn't just the hair on the back of Jack's neck that had risen. She was covered in gooseflesh and felt sick at the bottom of her stomach.

"What the devil?" Jack muttered. He looked down at her and then in a switch, took her hand and pulled her over his shoulder, so she was hanging low on his back.

"Jack!" Her squirming didn't affect his hold on her in the least. "What are you doing?"

He didn't reply, but he climbed the stairs, bypassing their bedroom and heading up a second flight. Violet squirmed a little more, but she couldn't help but laugh. She looked back down the stairs and found Hargreaves, staring after them with a wide grin on his face instead of his usual impervious expression.

He walked into the ballroom, not putting her down until they reached the center. She gasped as he slid her to the floor. The entirety of the ballroom was surrounded by hundreds of candles—tall, short, in candelabras and or on porcelain plates on the floor. The wireless was already playing her favorite jazz music. To the side of the room, there was a small table where champagne was sitting in an ice bucket, and she could see a tiered tray of small sweets. She had little doubt they'd be her favorite, bite-sized sweets.

"Jack—" Violet breathed. "It is magical."

He lifted her hand to him and then pulled her into a

dance. The tension of what they'd found in the parlor faded as he spun her around the floor, and despite the lingering sense of discomfort, she focused on what she loved. Him, their home, real love, and the happiness that was her life. Even when things were blue, she recognized how lucky she was. When things were good, as they had been lately, she was astounded by how blessed her life was.

CHAPTER 2

"*W*hat the—" Jack snapped his mouth closed, not moving to take the flowers from the delivery boy's hands.

Violet peeked around Jack's shoulder to see the bouquet. After the day before's red iris and today's Rose of Sharon, Jack had moved from maybe to certainty that whoever was sending these things wanted Violet's returned devotion. He took the bouquet and threw it, and the delicate lavender petals lay torn against the brick sidewalk.

"Oh Jack," Violet murmured.

He turned on her, furious, but she knew it wasn't directed at her. "Do you know what those things mean?"

She did, but she had also seen the flower language dictionary in his jacket pocket. She didn't answer as she knew he needed to get the rage out.

"Vi! Red iris means that he burns for you."

She handed the poor delivery boy a full pound note and

jerked her head for him to flee. He looked at her with gratitude and ran down the path and out the gate.

Jack cursed and then grumbled, glaring at the tattered blossoms. "That one means that they're consumed by their feelings for you."

Violet glanced back to Hargreaves, who watched them both with his even expression, but his gaze was as worried as Violet's. She left Jack in the doorway and asked Hargreaves, "Perhaps something calming. Chamomile? Hot milk?"

Jack growled at her, and she laughed, trying to lighten the tension as she bypassed the parlor where it was possible to see the front door and headed for the library instead. Jack paced behind her with the furious grace of a panther. Violet turned and asked, "Should we go to the zoo?"

He frowned at her, still fixated on the flowers he left on the walkway for Hargreaves to deal with. "Maybe we should return to the country."

Violet shook her head. She had a meeting that required her attendance with her man of business. Most of the time, her former maid, Beatrice, could take over for Vi but not this time. "I have that meeting on Monday."

Jack glanced at her with a look that said she was in charge of arranging such things. She was, of course, and she could reschedule, but it was foolish to be chased away from her home because of flowers. She flopped into one of the chairs near the fire and asked Hargreaves as he passed the library to have coffee and a tray of sandwiches sent in with Jack's tea.

"Why don't we go to Algie's party tonight?"

"I don't know, Vi—" Jack looked at her with that same worry-filled gaze that was starting to haunt her at all times.

"We can't be imprisoned because of a...a...bit of puppy love, Jack."

"And if it's something more? I know you've been thinking of Harriet as well."

Violet had been. Of *course* she had. The poor girl had received letters that showed far too much interest in her every movement and behavior. Harriet had decided to leave her village, and she'd been punished by strangling. The fellow had then turned his attentions to Violet's sister-in-law, Kate. It was only after both Violet and Kate had been injured that they'd caught the fellow.

"That doesn't mean that someone thinks the same way about me, Jack." Violet would have crossed her fingers to show her hope, but she knew that Jack would latch onto her instincts. The truth was that something wasn't right and her concern had been growing steadily for days. She'd come to flinch at the ringing of the doorbell.

She didn't want to work counter to her husband, she thought suddenly.

What was she doing? Trying to allay his fears and hiding her own?

"Jack," she said quietly. "I *am* spooked. But I'm also concerned that if we leave, he'll either simply follow or pop up again when we're least expecting it."

"He's trying to not be caught." Jack ran his hand over the back of his neck and then rose. This time it was he who was pacing and Violet who was watching. "Hargreaves and then Smith visited flower shop after flower shop. He comes in with his hat low, thick spectacles, and leaves a false name with the shop. He's used a different shop every time. It's maddening."

Violet fiddled with her wedding ring until the coffee arrived, and then she poured herself a large cup, breathing in the fumes, and considering on what they should do.

"Jack, there has to be a way for us to find this fellow. We've found murderers. This is just a—I don't know— nothing more than an unwanted flower sender. As much as he bothers me and brings to mind bad memories, all we truly have for certain is flowers with no name on the card."

Jack frowned, but he nodded. "Well, let's go to Algie's party, shall we? We can listen to your fool of a cousin who will probably tell you there is nothing to worry about."

"Is Ham back?" Violet asked and then winced when Jack shot her a dark look. "Not because I don't trust your opinion. I just thought you'd feel better to bounce ideas off of him." And to join them at the party as another set of eyes, just in case she was being followed, too. That was an unnerving thought.

Jack hooked the back of her neck and pulled her forward to kiss her forehead. "Nothing will happen to you."

"How could it with you looking after our family so carefully?"

"I CAN'T SEE that there's anything much to worry about," Algie giggled as his wife twirled with one of the members of the jazz band. The poor man had taken a break. He probably needed a drink and a smoke, and Clara had dragged him into a fast dance with the fringe on her dress flying.

"I regret my dress," Violet said, glancing down. It was tucked close to her body, a deep purple with black beading that created a slithering snake made of shimmering beads at the hem of her dress. It did not, however, have any fringe.

"She does look fabulous, doesn't she?" Algie agreed. "I'm a lucky man."

"You are," Violet said. "She's far too witty for you."

"She likes my joy." Algie shook his head and his giggle had Violet grinning in return. "Come meet all my friends, Vi love. You'll feel better in the end."

Violet winked at Jack and let her cousin pull her into the crowd. The moment they were away from Jack, Algie demanded, "Where is Victor? Why isn't he here when we're rallying round our Vi?"

"Kate is so sick." Vi shook her head. "I won't add to his burden."

Algie lifted a brow and then swung her in a circle as if they were turning in a dance before he bellowed, "My fellows! Come! Meet my cousin."

Algie glanced at Violet. "Surely you know Preston Bates?"

Violet followed Algie's gaze and she shook her head. He was taller even than Jack but rail slim. Vi was sure she'd never met this Preston before, but then she noticed a rather large mole on his jawline. It had to be the size of a sixpence coin. "Oh! I do remember his face," she murmured quietly to Algie, then louder as the man joined them. "It's been so long."

"I believe I knew your brother," Preston said. "Not sure we've ever been introduced." He held out his hand and Violet started to take it, but he had a red iris in his buttonhole. She paused and then fluttered like a silly woman to cover for the hesitation. "Oh! Excuse me. I see my husband waving."

Before he could stop her, Violet hurried back towards Jack with Algie at her heels.

"Vi!" Algie called, but she didn't stop until she was safely hooked through Jack's arm.

"What is wrong?" her husband asked, eyes already narrowing.

"I'm not going to tell you," she told him flatly.

"Why?" His demand was dark and furious.

"Because," Violet snapped back. "I already almost lost you to suspicion of murder. I won't lose you to actual murder."

Violet's cousin caught up with them, and Algie heard Violet. "What? Preston? He's a harmless old dog."

"Algie, you idiot!" Violet hissed.

Jack was all steel before he heard the name, but his careful gaze was moving about the room, and Violet could tell when it landed on that bedamned red iris. "Is that—"

But he didn't need the question answered. They knew all too well what a red iris looked like and what it meant.

"Is that what?" Algie squeaked. "Why does Jack look like he's going to murder someone? Is this about the flowers?"

"Algie," Violet hissed, "I need you to shut up."

Jack muttered, "This is where we should be looking for your flower man. I was thinking it could be anyone. Em's articles on you could have triggered some mad man to obsess. But these people, they've known you tangentially since you were a child. If there is a long-lasting interest, this is where we'll find it." Jack's gaze narrowed again on Preston Bates.

"Preston is a good chap," Algie argued. "Maybe don't kill my friend, please."

"You ask him right now," Jack said, "why he's wearing that flower."

"The flower?"

Jack's barely controlled rage had Algie holding up his hands in surrender.

"Of course," Algie said. "Of course. The flower. Let me talk to Preston. You take your murderous husband that way, Vi."

Violet caught sight of Algie's wife, Clara, and told Jack, "We need to say hello."

Jack glanced back, gaze narrowed. "What are the chances?"

Vi shook her head.

"Did anyone know we were coming?"

"Well, Algie," Violet said. "We can trust him."

"He's an idiot."

Violet shook her head and then Clara turned and Vi shifted her expression to one of delight. "Clara! I'm so happy to see you again."

"Oh," Clara grinned. She was a pixie of a woman with blonde hair, delicate features, and an effervescent grin. Her fringed dress spun as she moved, and she moved almost incessantly. "May I introduce you to my friends? This is Barnaby Gallagher, Mylo Hunt, and Roman Johnson. This," Clara said, gesturing to two women, "is Heather Johnson, Roman's wife, and my good friend, Winnie Cole."

Violet nudged Jack into greeting all of them as Winnie said, "Clara has told me all about you. Algie's clever cousin. I fear I have been quite shouting you from the roof tops. Detective Violet Wakefield!"

"Me?" Violet asked. "No, no. There's no reason for that. Anything that we found, killer or not, was more than just me. Jack, my twin, our friends. We all helped each other."

"Sometimes you even hire professionals, don't you?" That was from Barnaby Gallagher.

"Jack is a professional," Clara laughed. "Careful now or you'll have the Yard man on your trail."

"But you aren't really a Yard man," Mylo said. "Real Yard men take regular cases. You're a…rich man pretending at the Yard."

Violet gaped, clutching at Jack. His mood had been furious even before Mylo's rude asides pushed him beyond. Vi shot Clara a look, who winced and then said, "Don't listen to them, Jack dear. They're just jealous of men who have wits and skills."

"And money," Winnie shot out with a grin. "Lovely wife. Nice home. Algie looks up to you like an ancient Greek hero. These fools are emasculated around a real man like you, Jack."

"Oh it's a love story!" Roman said. "I've a beautiful wife." He tugged his Heather closer to him and pressed a kiss on her cheek. "I've money. We're not all jealous of Algie's hero."

Violet tossed them all a daggered look before searching for an escape. Algie was approaching with Preston, who glanced at Jack like he was a madman with a gun. She gave Jack a gentle tug, gave the others a quick nod, and retreated.

Approaching carefully, Preston spoke quietly so only Violet and Jack could hear. "The flower arrived just before I left with a note."

"What did it say?" Jack asked, but Preston pulled the note out of his pocket.

"With utter admiration."

Preston blushed, looking abashed. "My mum was a woman who knew about what flowers meant. I thought I might have an admirer." His tone read possible lover, but Violet and Jack let the man have his pride. "I had no idea I was going to be someone's chump."

Jack shook hands with Preston in a show of peace. "I wonder if you might let me take you out for lunch tomorrow."

Preston nodded, his gaze settling on Violet and then back to Jack. "Happy to, my friend."

Jack nodded and then pulled Violet with him onto the floor. He held her tightly as they danced, and Violet didn't need him to explain that any chance of having a light evening had fled, if there had been a chance to begin with. They didn't need to speak to know each was calculating how the spook knew they'd come to this party. Violet and Jack didn't come to all of Algie's parties. Was it just happenstance? Was the fellow prepared for every party? What was the point here? Why did he send that flower to Preston if not to manipulate them?

Jack spoke first. "Why would this fellow want to disguise himself if he's not of ill-intent?"

Vi shook her head. She had been bothered before. The flowers, the ring. But this…she'd have nibbled on her bottom lip or paced if they were at home. She didn't like any part of this. Not any of it. Jack had already been on edge, but she suspected that he'd be attached to her side until this was over. She pressed up and kissed his chin, little caring they were on the dance floor.

"Let's go home."

"Are you afraid?"

Vi shook her head. Not with Jack there. She wasn't afraid in the least. Disturbed yes, but entirely unafraid.

CHAPTER 3

"*L*et's get our coats," Jack said, his hand on Violet's arm as though he were going to haul her around like a recalcitrant child. She didn't take it amiss, however, given that he had the tight jaw, the alert gaze, and the careful maneuvering of a man who was moving through enemy lines.

Violet smiled at him as he pulled her gently after him, keeping her in the shadow of his body. If they were facing some sort of sniper situation, she'd be very safe indeed. He sent a servant to tell Hargreaves to pull their auto forward as Algie moved after them.

"Leaving so soon?" Algie's clear disappointment had Violet patting his arm with her free hand.

"I'm afraid that flower fiend has struck again and Jack is feeling a bit protective."

"Again?" Algie turned and scowled at the roomful of his friends and then looked back at Violet. "Shall we lock the doors and call the coppers?"

"And tell them what?" Jack snapped. "That some rogue is sending my wife flowers and I find it disturbing in the extreme? We'll be laughed out of London."

Algie cleared his throat and looked to the ground, blushing deeply.

"Jack has been through a rather large number of precarious situations," Violet told Algie flatly. "Where his instincts have kept him alive."

"I see, I see," Algie said amiably. "His instincts are screaming, are they? Like the soprano at the opera sort of situation. I understand. Have to admit I wouldn't love it if some blackguard were sending Clara flowers. Might set me to a bit of a rage." He giggled and then laughed harder at the look on their faces. "Don't believe me, do you? I might have a rage in me."

The servant who had gone for Hargreaves had appeared and was waiting silently to open the door. Jack noticed and nodded at Algie before pulling Violet under his arm.

"Jack," Violet said mildly. "I should like to keep my furs. I do so love them."

He paused and then let go of her while she gathered her coat from the girl. As Jack slid the coat up her arms, Violet tucked herself into the furs, letting the weight of the furs and Jack's ready arm warm her. She tucked her hands into the pockets against the chill and then frowned, slowly pulling out a rolled piece of paper.

Jack groaned as she unrolled it until her horrified gasp had him pulling it from her hand. It was a quick line sketch. The type of thing someone who had been educated by drawing masters could whip up. The lines formed Vi's face. If it were just her face, she wouldn't be bothered at all.

Instead, it was her entire body. In the drawing, she was sitting on a stool, twisted back to look over her shoulder. The artist had enough talent to put an expression of desire on her face. She was entirely starkers. Although the focus of the drawing was on her expression, it showed her spine, her bottom, the barest side curve of her breast.

Jack didn't react at all when he saw the drawing. She knew he didn't suspect her of cheating on him. There was no jealousy in his face. It was more an utter lack of response. She thought he might be having some sort of episode given that he only stared.

"What is it?" Algie asked, looking between them as if watching a tennis match.

Slowly—so very slowly—the tops of Jack's cheeks turned red. His gaze was fixed on the drawing, but when he turned to her, it was like he didn't know what to say.

"It's not me," she whispered.

"You?" Algie demanded. "I say now, let me see."

"I know, Vi." Jack's tone was a gentle though hoarse whisper.

"It isn't really my body." To her surprise, as violated as she felt, her need was to comfort him rather than herself. "This is just...fairy nonsense."

Jack turned so that Violet was blocked by everyone, including Algie, and then said low and even, "Violet darling, I have no concerns over where your heart is aimed. This—" He seemed to just keep himself from crumpling the drawing, and she was guessing it was some investigative rationale. "Even if you were clothed, Vi."

"Say what now?" Algie gasped.

Jack and Violet ignored Algie as Jack continued. "The

fellow knew which coat was yours, he knew your face well enough to draw it without you posing for him, he found a way to know we would be here and also to draw suspicions from himself with that trick with the flowers, assuming that Preston fellow can be believed. And all of that was before we saw the *way—*" Jack's anger was evident in the hoarse growl in his voice, "—he drew you."

Violet stepped into him and wrapped her arms around his body.

"How did he draw her? Is she…she's not…no one would draw another man's—my goodness." Algie muttered low and furious. "I say now."

The problem was when you laid it all out, nothing that had been done was something that Scotland Yard would be able to do anything about. There were no laws about drawing a picture of Violet. Not even if she was naked. Not even if she hadn't posed for it and didn't want it. There was no way to find this fellow and do anything other than scare him. Given the deadly fury that had covered Jack, however, Violet wasn't so sure that he would stop at only terrifying the man.

"Let's go home," Violet suggested.

"What are you going to do?" Algie demanded.

Jack's only response was to pull Violet down the steps to the house and into their auto.

JACK LAY NEXT TO VIOLET, but instead of the usual comforting presence, she felt a little like she was snuggling a statue. She would have been tossing and turning if she could sleep, but sleep was impossible knowing that Jack was awake and seething. The problem was...what were they supposed to do? Vi didn't want to feel like she couldn't walk her dogs to the park and be uncertain of whether someone was using that as a chance to draw pictures of her.

It didn't help that in all of the cases they'd come across, they'd experienced something like this before and of the man's victims, one hadn't survived. They couldn't help but think of Lila's cousin, Harriet, with her beautiful voice now lying in her grave.

Violet waited until Jack finally relaxed into sleep and then tiptoed from the room to pace in the hallway. She'd have taken a bath if it wouldn't wake him. At a moment like this, Epsom salts and lavender oil were just what she needed. A long lingering bath, possibly a glass of ginger wine while she soaked.

As Violet paced, she thought over the fellows that she'd seen at Algie's party. Her cousin's friends were all fellows she had *probably* known since she was young, even when they didn't linger in her mind as fellows that she knew. She considered back. Preston had taken her a long minute to remember, but she did know him. Barnaby, Mylo, and Roman, Violet might have met them a time or two over the years and the same could be said of the rest of that crowd at Algie's penthouse.

Vi fiddled with her wedding ring and glanced down when she heard a quiet whine. Her dog, Rouge, reliable angel that she was, followed Violet as she paced. It was comforting to not be alone, even at home.

Violet rubbed the back of her neck. Did she need to be afraid? It felt like she was one of the gazelles Rita talked about, being stalked by lions. Vi nibbled her lip and considered. Rita hadn't returned to London yet, but she wasn't trapped by a sick wife like her twin. It felt as though Victor and Kate, along with Lila and Denny, were out of commission. Rita, however—Violet would beg her to return to London in the morning.

Vi finally abandoned the hall for the room Lila used when she was in the house. Lila would have salts and oils and her room was far enough from Jack to let him sleep. After a long soak, Rouge lying nearby, watching her with worried, dark eyes, Violet crossed to the table in Lila's room and made a list of suspects:

Preston Bates - *Just because he said he had received the flower with a note didn't mean that it wasn't all a sham.*

Barnaby Gallagher —

Roman Johnson — Declared he was married and happy. Is it true? His wife was lovely, but men have been known to step out on those they love.

Mylo Hunt— Oddly abrasive to Jack.

Any of the other gents there — *Who's to say the fellow, whoever he is, wasn't just lurking in a corner like a spider? The note-writer wants to send the message of love, devotion, and passion and has the wherewithal to do so, but surely he knows that his actions are unacceptable? Why try to so hard to hide his identity if she didn't know him?*

Vi WOULD HAVE GIVEN a lot to talk to her twin about these names. No one else on the planet would be better able to tell her if she knew these men. What about Tomas? But no, Violet shook her head. Her brother-in-law might have been close to them long ago, but after the war, he was in his own head too much to be aware of acquaintances that Violet couldn't remember either.

Did she dare to telephone her brother and ask him? Violet wanted nothing more than to walk down to the library where the telephone was housed and do so, but she couldn't do that to him. She'd never, *ever* make him choose between herself and Kate. Perhaps Vi should track down wherever Tomas and Isolde were? Vi was sure her step-mother was in London which meant that Isolde had taken her husband and child and fled as soon as humanly possible.

Vi read the list over again. There was *something* about the name Mylo Hunt. Why was it triggering a smidgeon of a memory? Or was it bothering her simply because she hadn't liked him all that well?

Vi had *no* idea if any of the gents on the list were the fellow who seemed determined to drive her stark raving mad, but they were a place for Smith to start. Along with a guest list, if Algie had one. Time to start narrowing down who this fiend was before she found herself being yanked into a dark corner by a noose.

Vi rubbed the back of her neck again and then started when the clock gonged. It was 4:00 am, and she needed to return to bed and pretend to sleep before Jack rose. When she crawled back into the sheets, she prayed not to wake him, but the moment she curled onto her side, Jack pulled her close.

Neither of them spoke, even though they had both spent

the night worrying separately. Instead, Violet turned to face him, tucking herself close to hear her favorite lullaby, his heartbeat and the sound of his breathing. As she relaxed into his warmth, she slipped into an unexpected peacefulness and then into sleep.

CHAPTER 4

*W*hen Violet woke, she was no longer curled into Jack. On her side of the bed, however, was another presence. She turned slowly over with a sly smile, expecting Jack had gotten up and then returned to find her monopolizing his usual side of the bed.

The face that met hers had the same dark eyes, the same sharp features, and the same exhausted look of a night of little sleep.

"Victor!"

She tackled him and found that he clutched her almost as desperately as she clutched him.

"What are you doing here?" Her gasp had his gaze narrowing.

"Why didn't you call me?"

"I—" She bit down on her bottom lip. "Kate—"

"Violet Carlyle Wakefield," her twin shouted, taking her by the shoulders and shaking her lightly before he hugged her tightly again. "You drive me to drink."

She laughed, but her eyes welled with tears, which only seemed to set him off further. He muttered low and darkly about the idiocy of sisters and the foolishness of women, phrases that would never normally come from his mouth. Vi pinched him hard and then hugged him back.

"I missed you," she confessed. "How did you know?" It was no longer an accusation but a breathy exclamation of wonder.

"Algie telephoned, of course. Overwrought and declaring that Jack was going to murder half the town. I loaded the nanny, the twins, and Kate into the auto. We drove all night."

Violet gasped and then her own dark muttering began.

"It's fine," Victor told her. "Kate is better this time. Her nanny said that many women are very ill the whole time they're expecting, but it's often worse when there's more than one bun in the oven. I guess I wasn't an overachiever this time."

Violet elbowed him and then shuffled back to lean against the headboard of her bed next to him. "So Kate's not sick?"

"She is," Victor said. "Just not as much. The nanny knows all kinds of tricks that help. She's an angel straight from heaven, our Nanny Jane. Kate's endlessly swilling concoctions and eating to the woman's orders, but she doesn't mind. Better to consume loaves of dry toast and pitchers of ginger tea than to be sicking up."

Violet laid her head on his shoulder. "And my babies?"

"Giants," Victor said. "Vivi is just like you. Agatha just like Kate. Thank the heavens I only have one devil to deal with outside of you."

Vi grinned. She wanted to race out and scoop them up, but instead she stayed with her twin. Whenever they were separated, despite being married, she felt as though she'd lost a limb. She'd turn to speak to him or to meet his gaze and share a private glance, and he wasn't where he was supposed to be.

"Thank you for coming."

He was the one who elbowed her this time. "Not that you'll ever experience this again, but if there is a problem in the future and you don't send for me, I will wring your neck and put us both out of our misery."

Violet nodded resolutely and then asked, "Where's Jack?"

"He left for Smith and Ham. You should get dressed, my devil. They'll be back soon and Hargreaves has set the cook to make a meal of monumental proportions."

Violet rose to find her list of names and her note for Rita and found that they were gone. She frowned for a moment and then muttered, "Jack—" They were coming back, she could steal her list back then. "Who else is coming?"

"Denny is catching a nap. Lila has joined him."

"They're here?" Vi gasped. "How? When?"

"Obviously, I telephoned them before I left. They might be halfway to useless, but they'll gather what wits they have and employ them fully for you. And keep you entertained."

"Ouch," Violet said, wincing for their friends, and then she laughed. "They weren't even here to experience the shots fired."

"Well—" Victor shrugged, tugging her hair. "One should remain in practice."

"I have missed you all so much," Vi confessed. "It's not fun to be in London without you."

Victor shot a look that declared her idiocy. "I telegrammed Rita. Expect her soon if she isn't on the way already. I'm sure Jack has been keeping Ham filled in. Our boy Ham may well have called her back yet."

Violet scoffed and Victor gave her a surprised look. "Not *Ham* or Jack for that matter," Vi laughed. "These old school, honorable chivalric types don't tell their loves about a possible danger and then call them home. The last place Ham wants Rita is by my side if this fellow is as crackers as he seems."

Victor blinked in surprise and Violet's condescending look had him flushing. "If it were Kate—"

"I brought her," he said defensively.

It was the defensiveness that gave him away. "You tried to leave her, didn't you?"

"She's been unwell," he tried, but the attempt was so lame even he had to laugh. "Of course I tried. I was tempted to just leave and send her a telegram, but you've trained me better than that. I did, however, bring her a purse-sized pistol and make her practice using it while the maids were packing our things."

Violet could have laid her head on his shoulder and listen to his stories all day, but the babies were in the house, her best friends Lila and Kate were in the house, and Jack would be returning with his best friend along with all of his worries.

She slowly pulled away from her twin, but he stopped her with a single question. "Are you afraid?"

Vi looked back, meeting the gaze that never required anything of her but herself. "I don't know. It feels foolish to be scared, but I'm spooked. I'm disgusted. I'm—" Vi shook her head and then scrubbed at her eyes before returning to fiddle with her wedding ring. "I feel like eyes are on me even now, and I know that's in my head, so how can I follow my instincts? My imagination has come to play, and I hate that it seems like someone has been watching me and I never knew."

Victor frowned fiercely and his voice was so gentle as he asked, "I understand the drawing of you was quite—"

"Explicit?" Vi snapped, fury filling her. "Naked?" Her eyes filled with tears. "I feel—"

Victor waited, but Violet didn't know how to describe it. It wasn't like she posed for that drawing. It was only lines on the paper. It wasn't even her body. Her curves were different and she had a freckle at the top of her hip, and whoever drew that didn't have access to that fact. But someone had framed those lines to seem like her body and they'd topped it with her face, and she *hated* whoever had done that to her.

"Vi?" Victor asked. He stood and crossed around to her, but she rose, unable to be still.

She paced around her room and then admitted, "I don't know how I feel, Victor. I have a hundred feelings and they all are mixed up with madness and fury and a dash of horror, but mostly it just feels as though a ghost has invaded my house and is haunting me, and I don't know why. I haven't tried to attract some other man. I don't even know what I did."

"No one thinks you're trying to attract someone, Vi."

"Then why, in a world full of women, would someone turn their attention to me? I'm in love and happily married to the only man I want."

"I don't know, Vi, but I heard you once tell Isolde she wasn't responsible for the feelings men had towards her. You did say that, didn't you?"

Vi shot him a look that demanded he stop being so logical.

Her brother laughed. "Don't like having your own words thrown back in your face? It wasn't you in that drawing, Vi. You didn't even know that something was odd until the first flowers arrived, am I right?"

Vi nodded.

"How could any of this be your fault? This is the work of some deranged madman, I think. Nothing more than that."

Violet took a deep breath in and then nodded. "I know you're right. I suppose I'm being melodramatic, but in all the ways I imagined my life going, I would never have thought that this would happen to me. Since I haven't imagined it up, I don't know what to do."

Victor tugged a lock of her bobbed hair and grinned at her. "Don't worry, darling. You'll rally."

Vi grinned at him. "Well, I only slept a few hours last night. You know that makes me maudlin."

"I didn't sleep at all and you don't see me simpering." Victor's evil grin made Violet smack his arm, but there was something about that familiar grin that brightened her mood immeasurably.

Violet winked at her brother and crossed to her dressing room. For a day that involved a new kind of crime and the fabulous return of friends, she needed just the right dress. She'd be damned, after all, if she allowed this fiend to ruin her happiness at her family reuniting.

She was in no mood for one of her blush or nude dresses. She ignored those as much as she loved them. For several moments, she considered a flowered dress with a black sheer overlay. The flowers barely showed through the black, giving it a sort of darkness, like a garden at midnight. There was the mustard and black dress. The mustard top half ended with a tie around the hips and the black portion would flutter around her calves, but the black wouldn't do.

Violet frowned and then her eyes landed on a red dress. The sheer sleeves reached to her wrists, and the hem just below her knees. There were slightly darker red flowers on the fabric and it was belted just below her chest. Violet chose nude stockings with a seam that she straightened along the back of her leg. She added her favorite red t-strap shoes with diamond buckles.

It was a dress that demanded the world to look at her. If she was going to be observed from a distance by some fiendish man who wanted to send messages without attaching a name or a face, she wasn't going to hide. She added her black pearls from her twin, her spider ring, her favorite diamond and gold bangles and then finished with black pearl earrings.

Violet carefully took a seat at her vanity and powdered her face, kohled and added mascara to her eyes, completing the look with a bright lipstick to match her dress. When she was done, she looked ready for more than a day of breakfast with friends, but she felt better, like she had reclaimed the part of herself the nameless fiend had tried to steal for himself.

Violet crossed to take up her journal, her favorite pen, and considered. Jack had left the drawing behind. She could see it rolled up on the table near the fireplace. She wanted to throw it in the fireplace even though it hadn't been lit. Instead, however, she slowly took it up. She wasn't going to hide from any part of this. She couldn't make this person turn away from her, but she could work with her friends to ferret him out and give him a firm and clear declaration of her thoughts.

Flowers that meant passion? Drawing her like he had? Discovering where she was going to spend her time and ensuring that she knew he was there and watching? She wasn't going to have to worry about Jack murdering the fellow. She may well take care of it herself.

CHAPTER 5

"Violet, darling!" Denny said as she entered the breakfast room, standing to kiss her on each cheek. "I have missed you like the days are long. I have missed you like the sky is blue. I have missed you, devil, who has driven some poor man mad and without me near."

Violet laughed at the cheery face, but she kissed his cheek back for the worry in his eyes. "To distraction, perhaps. I don't think he's quite so mad as he seems. Did Lila take away your chocolate?"

"She did!" Denny patted his larger stomach and then laughed. "She had been making me walk with her, but—"

"But I got too fat, darling. How I love you." Lila grinned from her seat and Violet crossed to kiss her cheek.

Vi also kissed Kate's cheek, noting the pallor beneath her happiness, but she wasn't quite so horrifically thin this time and she wasn't quite so horrifically swollen in places.

"Kate—" Vi started.

Kate waved off the words. "Don't worry, love. It really is

better this time. I'll be feeling absolutely ravenous before long. Until then...ginger tea and toast."

Vi grinned at Ham sitting nearby, and then accepted the cup of Turkish coffee that Jack handed her as she took her seat. "Tell me, Ham, when is the wedding date?"

"June," Ham said. "I've been having her father distract her, but I believe my tricks have been found out."

"Keeping her safe from me and my madman?" Vi asked lightly. "She won't love that."

Jack shot Violet a dark look and amended, "*The* madman."

"Oh ho," Denny laughed, clapping Jack on the back of his shoulder. "Jealous, old man? Violet's heart isn't swayed."

"I wonder if there has been a woman where this type of thing worked." Lila sipped her tea and then moaned, "Oh, I am so fat."

"What do you mean?" Victor asked. "Some lady gets flowers and obscene pictures and thinks, '*someone likes me*'?"

Victor's scoff had both Violet and Denny laughing but Ham lifted his brows as he confessed. "I knew a woman just like that once. I worked the early case. Terrifying little affections left on her doorstep. When he finally revealed himself, she just gave in."

"Never!" Kate said in ringing tones. "Where was her spirit? Her pride?"

"Well," Ham countered, "she wasn't as spirited and kind as our Vi. Nor did she have so many friends. Or any friends for that matter."

"It makes me shudder." Violet shook her head over her cup of coffee. "I can't imagine such a terrible outcome. What happened to her?"

Ham shook his head. "I kept an eye on her for as long as I could, but they eventually moved."

"Was she happy before she left?" This question was Kate and the thread of hope conveyed all of their thoughts except for Ham.

He shook his head. "She was quite wan. She'd never say one way or the other, but I fear my hopes have been thin indeed."

Violet sighed and then declared, "Victor, darling. This calls for chocolate cocktails."

"Dear heaven, please," Denny breathed. "Violet, say you have a box of chocolates."

"Of course, I do," she assured him, and they all looked at Lila who rolled her eyes and shrugged.

"It won't just be him who needs to shed a few stone after this baby arrives. I'll be damned if I lose my wardrobe to thicker hips."

Vi laughed and then paused, horrified, when she realized she was tearing up.

"Vi?" Jack asked, noting it immediately. When everyone turned her way, she flinched and Victor laughed.

"Not enough sleep and happy to have everyone back, pretty devil?" Victor rose. "This does call for cocktails."

"Well now—" Denny stood and loaded his plate with some of the mountain of food before returning to the table. "I want to hear about the suspects. Who are they? Lurking about the bushes, what? I suppose Jack has called in the louts who watched the house after that little shrew pranked you to near madness."

"The louts from last time are too obvious this round. We've hired some of Smith's friends and put them in as servants."

"We have?" Violet asked and then elbowed Jack. "You could have told me."

35

"My beautiful Violet," Jack shook his head, "you'd have guessed if you weren't thinking about other things."

Vi drained her coffee and then turned to Jack. "That's not nice."

"You've been distracted trying to figure this out alone. Let's work on it together."

Violet faced her friends. "Jack has the names. I think I might know them. They niggle at my mind, but I can't place it."

"Well," Lila said lazily. "You are sometimes half in your head with your stories. Especially in those early days when you actually needed the money to eat and buy stockings."

Jack pulled out Violet's list and read:

Preston Bates - *Just because he said he had received the flower with a note didn't mean that it wasn't all a sham.*

Barnaby Gallagher —

Roman Johnson — Declared he was married and happy. Is it true? His wife was lovely, but men have been known to step out on those they love.

Mylo Hunt— Oddly abrasive to Jack.

Any of the other gents there — *Who's to say the fellow, whoever he is, wasn't just lurking in a corner like a spider? The note-writer wants to send the message of love, devotion, and passion and has the wherewithal to do so, but surely he knows that his actions are unacceptable? Why try to so hard to hide his identity if she didn't know him?*

"Let's start with the first, Preston. What's all this about a flower?"

Jack explained about the bouquets that had been arriving and the meaning of them.

"Wait now," Denny cut in. "Did you discover the meanings of these bouquets or did you know them already?" The humor in his tone had Jack shooting him a dark glance.

"I bought a book. For example," Jack told Denny, "perhaps I might give you a yellow carnation."

"I feel like that joke definitely went right over my head."

"It means disdain," Kate told him, trying to hide her grin.

"There is my beautiful fox," Victor said, rising to get her more tea. "Smarter than the rest of us combined."

"The flower that Preston was wearing," Violet continued, "matched the bouquet that had been sent just this week. I didn't recognize him at first. I needed to take note of that large mole on his jawline."

"Oh yes, I remember him," Denny muttered. "Once tried to persuade Lila from my side."

"He didn't want me long term," Lila said easily. "Or I might have been tempted. I understand he had quite a nice income coming his way."

Denny grabbed his heart but Victor cut in. "I remember Preston. A rower, I think. He played poker with Algie and Theo."

"I don't like him," Lila said instantly. "Theo. Agh. I don't want to talk about that murdered snake again."

"What about Mylo Hunt?" Violet asked. "Why do I remember that name?"

"Oh my goodness!" Lila laughed. "I remember him. He

was in school with Denny and Victor and Tomas. Oh! When we were about twelve years old? Surely you remember?"

"Yes!" Denny clapped his hands together. "He used to lag after us. He had some scheme he was always trying to get us in on. What was it about?"

"Tomas will remember," Victor said. "He was kinder than Denny and I ever were. He might have actually engaged in that scheme."

"Well," Violet said with a sigh, "I suppose we must have known him since we were forever lagging after the boys ourselves, Lila."

"They were lagging after us." Lila shot Denny a look that said he had better agree.

"Of course," Denny answered instantly, but his wicked grin said he was indulging his wife, and they all knew him well enough to read that expression.

"Surely, it's too much to think that there's some long-lingering passion that has lasted since that time." Violet glanced at her husband. "Even if he did seem to despise Jack."

"If I recall the rumors," Lila said, "he's had a few interactions with the law. Perhaps that's why he decided to go on the attack. Jack was the symbol of his enemy."

"It doesn't matter," Violet said, finally ready for something to eat. She rose and took fruit and toast, bypassing the eggs but selecting slices of the bacon. "What about the others?"

"I know Roman Johnson," Kate said and they all turned to her at once. "What? Just because I was home with my mother all the time doesn't mean I've never met anyone."

"You met me, you lucky thing," Victor told her. "Fate took a hand."

"Yes, well," Kate said, nudging Victor. "Fate took a hand previously and I met Roman. I know his wife, Heather, too."

"Are they in love as they seem?"

"Not like you and Jack," Kate said.

Victor groaned. "Darling, you wound me."

"Or even like Lila and Denny, who perplex us all with their devotion."

"One isn't able to understand the depths of our passions," Denny declared.

"The only passion you have is for chocolate, old man," Victor told him.

"Let's focus here," Jack said and Ham nodded. "Ham and I have no idea of your old tales. Kate, you know Roman and his wife. Are they truly devoted?"

"I have no idea, really," Kate answered. "I have met them is all. Heather Johnson's grandmother lives near my mother. I've just been to garden parties with them."

"Do you know anything else?" Ham asked.

Kate shook her head. "No, unfortunately. I probably should. Before I met you, I spent my days reading and not listening to my mother's gossip. I was very good at the 'mm-hmm.'"

"You still are, darling Kate," Victor said.

Lila laughed. "All women are. Aren't I right, Vi?"

Vi choked on a laugh. "Too bad your mother isn't here to tell us all that gossip you ignored. Dear Kate, I regret your uplifted mind."

Jack sighed. "Kate, there was gossip?"

"I believe so," Kate said. "I have no idea, however, what it was about. For all I know, it could have been about having eaten all of the cake at the soiree. Our amusements were thin indeed."

"We've saved you, sweet Kate." Denny handed her another dry piece of toast as Victor accepted the ingredients for their favorite cocktails from Hargreaves. "Don't think back on those days."

Kate scoffed and took the glass of iced ginger beer from Victor as he went to work on the chocolate cocktails.

"Shall we set aside the investigation and get zozzled?" Victor asked brightly as he shook the ingredients up.

"Barnaby Gallagher!" Lila said suddenly. "Dark hair? Bit thick about the middle? Something of too-broad nose?"

"Ah," Violet breathed in. "Yes. A little thick, I suppose."

"He favored quite bright colors."

"He was wearing a brilliant yellow shirt," Violet agreed. "It wasn't quite the thing for his skin tone. You know him?"

"He's a rogue," Lila declared firmly. "And that's coming from me. I feel sometimes that I must ask myself, what would Violet do, before I am quite sure if I am behaving admirably."

"Why?" Ham demanded. "What makes him a rogue?"

"I'd tell you happily if I knew." Lila frowned and Vi could see from her expression that she wanted nothing more than to lay out the grisly tales while they sipped the cocktails Victor was handing round. "It's all asides. '*Watch out for that one.*' That kind of thing. I just avoided him as I'd been warned. It wasn't like I was interested in anyone other than Denny anyway."

"Well, I am a catch," Denny said.

"Especially once you start their training," Violet countered. "It's so much work to begin again."

Kate snorted as Lila lifted her glass. "Just so, my love."

"Or, of course," Ham said, taking the list from Jack and

looking it over. "It could be any number of fellows that we don't know to consider."

"Don't say such things, my lad," Denny groaned. "That makes all this a useless exercise, and I do so hate exercising."

"Oy." Victor tugged Violet's hair. "With all of us working together, Vi, we'll find the fellow, whether it's one of these gents or another."

CHAPTER 6

*V*iolet twirled outside of the house and then grinned as she looked over her shoulder at Lila and Kate.

"Do you smell that?"

"What?" Kate asked laughing. She was early days yet in this pregnancy and only showed the barest curve of her stomach. She seemed to be enjoying the scent of fresh air as well, but what she said was, "The smell? Who cares about the fresh air? It's the silence that's magical! No babbling. No squawking. I love my daughters with every inch of my soul, but my goodness—I don't think I've breathed since they were born."

"Well and there's no smell of dirty nappies either," Violet said. "But I swear, Jack has been hovering, and I've been feeling a bit smothered."

"If only Rita were here," Kate laughed as one of Smith's men approached with the auto. Hargreaves was driving while the extra man was sitting in the front passenger seat. "Do you think he's armed?"

"Yes," Violet replied.

"And Rita is on her way." Lila's lazy statement had both Violet and Kate gasping as the man got out of the auto and moved to open the door for them.

"How?" Kate asked.

"When one of those men of ours gets it in his pretty little head to protect us against our will, it's the responsibility of the others to nip it in the bud."

"Did you telephone her?" Vi demanded.

"I did. While you were fluffing your flashy dress and updating your lipstick. As a walrus, I felt little need to polish the cow, so to speak."

"You look lovely," Violet told her.

"I look clever and remarkably helpful." Lila's wicked grin was directed at the two of them and she nodded Kate into the car. "I'm not sliding across all those seats. I can barely lumber. Violet can have the middle seat."

"How were you helpful?" Kate slid across the seats followed by Violet and then Lila, who let the man hand her into the auto.

"I sent Rita to your mother," Lila said evilly. "She'll gather what there is to know and come down the next day on the train."

"Will she?" Kate asked. "Oh my. My mother will be thrilled to dig up old gossip. I'll have to somehow claim your sending Rita and use it to keep in good graces."

"In trouble are you?" Lila asked idly and then groaned. "This evil little monster is leaning on my bladder."

"I thought she was an angel," Violet shot back.

"She was until she found my bladder," Lila huffed. "At this

size, I could break a limb getting my stockings on. Having to adjust my clothing, with stockings, and slips and what not. Using the ladies is torture."

Violet laughed, but Kate reached over and took Lila's hand. "It just gets so much more uncomfortable until the end."

Violet laughed harder and they both shot her dark looks. In defense, she held up her hands and offered, "Ice cream on me?"

"Yes," Lila said. "Now come buy clothes and we'll look on in envy."

"You'll need bigger clothes," Kate told Lila. "You explode at the end. Unfortunately, I'll be able to reuse the same ones, and since I never intend on falling pregnant again, I might as well be frugal."

The auto stopped in front of Violet's favorite boutique. "Hargreaves, prepare yourself," Violet announced. "Kate, Lila, and I will be indulging ourselves madly."

Hargreaves nodded with a twinkle in his eyes on his otherwise impervious face. "Mr. Gold will wait outside of the shop, Mrs. Vi. I'll be nearby with the auto."

Vi could hear the worry in his tone, and she winked at him. He, more than anyone else, had seen the effect of these constant messages and gifts coming to them. The other servants weren't enough in their day-to-day lives. Even Violet's steady Beatrice had been taking a well-earned vacation and visiting her relatives. She wouldn't be back for a few more days, so only Hargreaves had been there to bear witness.

Mr. Gold, the man hired by Jack and Smith, opened the door for the ladies. This time it was Kate who was able to get out first and Lila had to sidle across the car seats regardless.

She almost rolled out of the auto before Violet caught her and propped her up until she was steadied.

"I'm not made for this," Lila declared, straightening her dress and then shooting Mr. Gold a dark look, as though it were his fault instead of him being merely the person who was holding the door.

"You don't have to come in," Violet told him.

He nodded, but entered the shop and walked through, making sure that all seemed well before he exited and stood outside.

"That was dramatic." Kate huffed a laugh and then asked, "Do you think that's what it's like to be royalty? They have to examine every place you go?"

"They probably have minions who buy things for them." Lila entered the shop and then sighed. "I have missed our shopping trips. And our everything. The country is boring without you, Vi."

"Kate is there." Violet examined a table where a jumper was draped becomingly over a small box filled with gloves.

"I'm not fun," Kate replied. "I've been sick as a dog until recently and now that I'm feeling better, I want nothing more than to revisit some of my favorite books."

"See." Lila eyed the shop girl. "Bring what you have for walruses. I'm prepared to throw away all of our money to drape this mound in something semi-fetching."

The girl nodded quickly, uncertain of how to reply, and glanced between Violet and Kate before darting to a solitary armoire at the back of the shop and pulling out some dresses for Lila. Violet wandered through the shop on her own, examining dresses. She was a huge fan of the nude and barely-there pink dresses that emphasized her slenderness and there were several, but she also *had* several already.

Instead, she pulled out an ice blue evening gown. It looked like nothing more than a swathe of fabric, but she could imagine it on her, so she handed it to the girl to set aside.

"Lady Violet," a woman said and Vi turned and found the designer. "I have been missing you. Yes, yes that dress is perfect, but do come try these."

Violet followed Jada to the dressing room and allowed herself to be helped into the ice blue dress. In a moment, Violet was certain that she loved it. It sparkled in the light and the deep cut to her chest would make Jack's jaw tighten. She laughed at the idea and then she spun in front of the mirror.

"Let us see," Kate demanded from the other side of the door. "Lila has taken a seat and refuses to try on the clothes that the poor girl got her."

"Oh," Violet laughed as she stepped out of the dressing room, following Kate down the small hall, and then finding her way to the trifold of large mirrors near the seats. "We'll have to dress her ourselves, Kate."

"I already dress my daughters. I'm not dressing a full grown woman who's a little off-balance."

"You're mean," Lila said without heat. "I wouldn't dress me either. I'm just resting for a moment."

"Resting from the arduous job of driving over here?" Violet asked as she turned to examine the back of the dress in the mirror. It was cut low in the front and the back, and she was enchanted by the way it shimmered. "I just like sparkly things."

Kate laughed. It wasn't a mean sound, but it was a bit sarcastic. "Yes darling, we know. You're usually coated in diamonds."

Vi winked at Kate in the mirror and then told Jada, "This one, certainly."

"Certainly," Jada agreed. "There's quite a lovely black shimmering dress in the back. It's just come in with beading in the shape of dragons. I know how fond you are of them. I have the most wonderful staff of beaders and embroiders who are sheer geniuses."

"Mmm," Violet agreed, eyeing a silver headband nearby.

Jada carried on as she said, "I do think you'll just love it. I've also found—"

Vi held up a finger to make her pause and picked up the headband to settle over her dark hair.

"That does look nice, you...you...sylph." Lila rubbed her belly. "I do hate you when I'm massive and you're so thin."

"I might hate you when you have an angel and my arms are empty."

Lila scoffed. "Everyone knows that's on purpose, Vi."

Violet grinned and turned in the mirror again. "Certainly this one, Jada."

Kate took a seat next to Lila. "I find I'm missing the girls. I felt suffocated by them before and now it's like my arms ache for them. I am a mess."

"You're a woman who has been exhausted and sick for longer than a year. You just need your body to return to normal and maybe a few weeks in a row of sleeping through the night."

"You don't sleep through the night with a nanny?" Lila demanded.

"I can't sleep if the girls are too far away, and I can't sleep if they're crying. I just can't—" Kate accepted a cup of tea from the shopgirl. "It's terrible being a mother. I would never, ever go back to before, but it is a living horror at times."

"Oh." Lila looked at Violet with wide eyes and Vi laughed.

"You'll be fine of course," Kate said lamely. "Everything will be just fine."

"Too little too late," Vi advised mockingly. "Let's see that other dress, shall we?"

Violet followed Jada back to the dressing room and slipped behind the curtain, handing the dress out a moment later. The ice blue dress had required Vi to take off all of her underthings to see a proper fit. She'd need to buy something specifically for that dress.

She took the dress she'd worn in off of the hook to get her slip, but it wasn't there. Vi hissed and looked to the stool where she'd left the rest and found her stockings on the floor. She had absolutely left them on the stool with the rest of her underthings, but the stool was empty. She moved it aside even though she knew that her underthings wouldn't be there.

The lace and satin camisole, the lace and satin unmentionables...they were gone. Vi's hands started to shake. She'd been shopping in this shop from Jada for years. She'd left jewelry, her handbag, cash, all of those things in her dressing room and never had a problem with anything disappearing. And if they had, it wouldn't have raised the hair on her neck the way her missing underthings did.

"My lady?" Jada called. "Did you want to try the black dress?"

"Jada, someone was in here." Violet heard the shrill tone in her voice.

"Oh, I'm sure that can't be true," Jada said.

Vi opened the small door and stuck her head out. "My underthings are gone."

"I'm sorry?" Jada's gaped at Vi in incomprehension.

"My underthings are gone!" Vi hissed again. "Get Lila and Kate and get me something to put on."

"My lady," Jada began.

"Now, Jada. You can search later if you'd like but, you won't find them. Did you see anyone in here?"

"No," Jada said. "Of course I didn't. I wouldn't let someone rifle through your things, my lady."

"Jada," Violet growled. "I am feeling quite naked here. Please."

The woman nodded frantically and hurried away. She didn't return for far too long and when she did, Violet was approaching furious, but the white look on Kate's face was sufficient to have Violet cursing low.

"What?"

"There's a note." Kate handed over new underthings and then slipped in to help Vi dress. "I am unprepared to leave you alone."

"What did the note say?" Violet demanded as she put her stockings on.

"With emboldened passion." Coming from Kate's disgusted tone, it sounded so funny Violet snorted.

"Vi—" Kate's hushed tone had Vi looking up in horror.

"There was another drawing?"

Kate nodded.

"From the front this time?"

Kate was too quiet.

Violet looked up as she arranged her dress over her body. "Well?"

"It was you and Jack. Jack had an 'X' over his face and there was a shadowy figure behind you."

Vi stared. Slowly she started to put on her shoes, but her hands were shaking. "No."

"Vi—" Kate started, but Vi held up her hand.

"I can't right now, Kate." Vi's hands continued to shake as she glanced around the room and then she walked out, passing Lila, who was holding the offensive drawing. Vi could tell by the curl of the paper. She bypassed Jada and the shop assistant and then stumbled outside.

"Lady Violet!"

She looked back and saw Mr. Gold. Someone must have explained what had happened.

"Don't go outside right now. Wait while I figure out how he got in."

Vi turned away, shaking her head, and stepped away from the shop. She took a slow breath in and let it out in a shudder. A moment later, Kate and Lila followed.

"Violet, don't be foolish."

"I would say I can't breathe," Violet said, "but I can. I can breathe, and I can see, and I can move, and I can commit a murder of my own."

CHAPTER 7

"We can't just stand out here," Lila said. "You might be fired by rage and as slender as a tree, but as I have said, I am a walrus."

"You aren't worried about Jack?" Kate demanded.

"Jack? Jack Wakefield?" Lila laughed. "The man who lived through the Great War and has since been shot and stabbed? He's on high alert, he's a warrior, and he's certainly armed. I would pity the fool who attacked Jack, but I would much prefer that the fool attack, lose the fight, and we all go out for cocktails unimpeded."

Violet grinned weakly at Lila and then admitted, "That would be something. An out and out attack that failed horrifically, but who's to say that he'll have enough honor to strike head-on?" Violet glanced around to find Mr. Gold. "Did Gold call for Jack?"

Kate nodded. "We were ordered to remain."

Violet eyed her friends who both seemed as determined to leave simply because they'd also been ordered to remain.

BETH BYERS

"The cheek." Lila fluffed her hair, but she glanced behind her and her gaze was worried. Violet had noted the rolled drawing that was escaping Lila's handbag.

"As though Victor doesn't try to get away with that high-handedness, not sure I quite like taking it from some random man," Kate agreed.

"I suppose we should take into account the recent theft." Lila eyed Violet and then turned back to Kate and lifted both brows. Neither of them truly wanted to leave the safety of the attendant and it was all to protect Violet. She loved them for it.

"Then we'll go to the bookstore, so he doesn't lose his mind. I could use something to read when I don't sleep tonight. We'll be safe enough together, won't we?" Violet looked at Mr. Gold, who was staring at her in horror. She faced Hargreaves. "You'll come, won't you, my friend?"

"Of course, Mrs. Vi."

Violet put her arm through Hargreaves's and headed towards the bookstore.

"You're armed?"

"Of course, my lady."

"Are you a good shot?" she asked while Lila and Kate gaped.

"I have become proficient. Smith has been teaching me."

"Beatrice's Smith?"

"She is my niece, you know. He said as much trouble as you two get into, it would be best to have weapons at the ready."

Vi's eyes widened and then she laughed. "Oh, I do like you Hargreaves."

The bookstore wasn't one of those high-end locations where the posh usually shopped. Jada's perfect little boutique was in the up and coming side of London and half the shops were amazingly redone places and the other half were rough and tumble. This bookshop fell into the latter with cracked, yellowed windows and chipped paint. There were bars on the windows and a scent of moisture in the air that didn't bode well for the books that lingered in the shop.

"There is something remarkably soothing about a bookstore, isn't there?" Kate asked. She wove her arm through Violet's free one. "I think I'll get something on birds."

"Birds?" Lila scoffed. "Oh, if I'm going to read, it's detective stories, one of Vi's Twinning novels, or perhaps a salacious French novel."

"Maybe there's a new Tarzan to distract you," Kate suggested. "Ludicrous though they are."

"They're fun," Violet defended. "You're supposed to suspend disbelief like you do with those detective novels where the fellow comes across body after body."

"I do find those hard to believe," Kate said agreeably. "Which is why I think I'll get a book about birds. You know, they aren't quite the same in the south of England as they are near home."

"I did not know that," Lila replied. "Nor did I want to."

Vi laughed and tugged Hargreaves with her down an aisle. "Look," she said. "Look at this. It's my books. All in a row."

"I believe that Victor would object to the 'my.'" Hargreaves took one in his hands. "This is my favorite, Mrs. Vi."

Vi grinned at the cover with the spectre on it. "I did like that one." The book was based upon her sister, Isolde. She'd created the character to scold her sister for the foolishness of her first engagement and Isolde's having been manipulated out of living her life as she chose.

53

Another man entered the aisle where they were. Hargreaves stiffened and Vi patted his hand lightly. The man was youngish. Quite near Vi's age, which was setting off her alarms even though he might only be a random lad looking for an excellent book. He was handsome enough, but she really only appreciated Jack's looks these days. She was capable of seeing the fine arc of his nose and the square strength of his jaw, but it was rather like viewing a very fine statue.

"Are those the Twinnings novels?" the man asked. "I have been checking for a new one quite regularly." His eyes glinted at her, and Violet let Hargreaves tuck her farther back.

"Yes," Violet said, backing away with Hargreaves who angled himself in front of Vi. "My friend here quite enjoys the ones with the spectres."

"I like the ones with the sweet ingenue manipulated by her family."

"Do you? I always thought she was ridiculous myself."

"Oh no." He held out his hand. "Jude Brown. And I fear you are quite mistaken. Would you like to discuss it over tea?"

"Her husband wouldn't like that very much," Hargreaves said smoothly, with a perfectly even tone. "Come, Mrs. Vi. You've read all these."

"Vi? Not the Vi of the V. V. Twinnings? I am quite your biggest fan, and I have just realized why I recognize your face."

Vi took the man's hand when he offered it again, cautious but not wanting to put off a reader if his conversation was innocent. "Violet Wakefield."

"Once Carlyle?"

"Oh bloody hell," Lila said as she approached. "Kate! Vi is causing trouble."

"So many people to look after you, Lady Violet."

"Just Vi, please." She glanced to Lila. "They're all so protective."

"Do you need protecting?" The twinkle in his eye was enough to make Vi want to gag, but she smiled to hide her reaction.

"Just from myself. I'm ever diving into trouble, don't you know? How did you recognize me? The lovely part of being an author with a pen name is walking about in public and no one giving a fig who you are, especially for the tripe of V.V. Twinnings."

"I suppose your tripe appealed to some readers despite yourselves. But I recognized you because I know you already. Lady Violet Carlyle. We met at a party once. Years ago now, I'm afraid."

"Did you?" Lila asked lazily. Her gaze narrowed. "With Preston Bates. I remember your face with his."

Mr. Brown nodded. "Yes, yes. My cousin, you know. He drags me over to this part of town far too often. Nearly daily. It's why I've become so good at looking for your new book."

"It'll be a while yet," Vi told him. "My brother is still working on his part. You're cousins with Mr. Bates?"

"Our mothers are sisters." Mr. Brown grinned but then eyed her. "Why do you care?"

"I was reacquainted with your cousin just recently."

"Yes, at the party with Algie. I intended to hunt you up there. I admit my fingers were crossed that I'd meet your brother as well. I had imaginings that I would persuade you both to sign my books. I have them all."

"Did you?" The voice was Jack and they all started as he asked, "And who are you?"

The man held out his hand. "Jude Brown. One-time acquaintance of your wife, I believe. I saw you the other week, hovering over her like one of her spectres. In her books, I think you'd be the alarming husband that our heroine needs rescuing from."

Vi snorted. "Oh my, Mr. Brown, you are too bad. I assure you, I married my husband of my own free will."

His smile froze and he looked between them all and admitted, "Well, that sounded terrible when I reconsider my words. I only meant insofar as descriptions might go."

Vi poked Jack as he took her arm from Hargreaves. "You're the villain, darling."

"Am I?" He didn't sound nearly so amused.

Vi laughed harder at the sound of Jack's voice even though most of her humor was an act. She squeezed his arm, and she was sure he noticed how her fingers dug too deeply into his skin.

"Come, Vi," Jack said. "We have lunch with your father."

"Oh yes," Violet said. "Duty calls. So nice to meet you, Mr. Brown."

"Do call me Jude."

Jack's acting wasn't quite up to Vi's level and the dark look he cast Jude Brown had him hurrying out the door.

"It's him," Lila declared.

"Agreed," Kate added.

"I wouldn't be surprised," Vi admitted. "I just can't decide if I'm bothered by his presence because he came after what else happened or if my instincts are raising an alarm."

"I don't like any of this, Vi," Jack said.

"I don't like it either," she said. "I feel *dirty*."

"That you are not."

Hargreaves cleared his throat. "I fear I have additional information."

Jack groaned, pulling Violet into his arms. He pressed a gentle kiss on her forehead and then glanced at Hargreaves. "What do you know?"

"That face, sir. I sometimes walk the dogs in the morning when I'm not needed." Hargreaves glanced between them. "A walk, well—"

"Hargreaves, my dear man, by all means, walk the dogs daily and no one will be bothered. You're welcome to do that, of course!" Violet shivered in Jack's arms. Hargreaves was dedicated in every way. If he wanted to walk the dogs and breathe some fresh air, he was welcome to do it.

"I have seen that man in the park. With a few other men of a similar age. They have several dogs between them."

"Do they?" Lila breathed. "Are they little sweet spaniels like Vi's? That would be creepy."

"Bulldogs," Hargreaves replied. "That's a neighborhood park, Mr. Wakefield, Mrs. Vi. The local nannies take the children there. The residents are the only ones who visit our little green."

Jack cursed. He was statue-still against Vi once again. If things continued to proceed as they were, he was going to have a stroke.

"Speaking of curses," Violet said, shoving her worries aside. "We don't really have lunch with my father, do we?"

Jack chuckled. "I don't know how you make me laugh when I'm trying not to punch the wall."

Violet wound their fingers together. "It's a talent. I'm a joy to the world, you know. A woman like me is valuable beyond rubies. Faithful, loving, devoted. You , sir, are a rich man in your wife."

"Too true," Lila declared. "Too, too true."

"Let's leave," Jack groaned. "Let's go home and pretend that there isn't a fiend obsessed with you."

"Surely you're obsessed with me?"

Jack laughed. "Only on Wednesdays."

"Wednesdays? Why Wednesdays?"

"That's when you're the likeliest to avoid trouble. Weekends are a hazardous time to adore you, wife."

"Not fair," Lila argued. "We've learned that parties are dangerous places in these last years. They're almost always on weekends, you know. It's not Violet's fault."

"I think Violet is capable of getting into trouble on Wednesdays if she set her mind to it," Kate added.

"Please don't," Jack pled. "Please, darling Vi, don't put your mind to it."

"So this is my fault now?"

"No," everyone replied.

"Never." Jack kissed her on the forehead again and then once again on the tip of her nose.

CHAPTER 8

*J*ack wasn't going to pretend he wasn't furious. He wasn't the actor his wife was. And he wanted whoever the deranged man was stalking his Violet to know just how very furious he was.

So while the ladies were seeing to Kate's twins, he stood staring out the parlor window with the men present.

"What did Gold have to say?" Ham paced in front of the fireplace until Victor placed a cocktail in his hand. "He didn't see anything? What kind of second rate fools did Smith pawn off on us?"

"Blackberry and mint with an excess of gin. Don't get too zozzled," Victor ordered, "because we need your wits here to catch this fellow before Vi stops teeter-totting between spooked and amused and lands on indignant."

"Indignant?" Ham asked. Cocktail in hand, he paced and sipped. "Taking her underthings…that's just—I'm more than indignant myself."

Jack bristled but kept silent.

"Perhaps infuriated is the better word," Victor amended. "Vi has been laughing this off for a while, but that drawing with Jack's face? That's not going over well. Once she thinks on it too long? Well, she's Vi. Think about how Rita might react if she became infuriated."

Ham winced.

"Speaking of Rita—" Denny sniffed. "I believe we'll be seeing her quite soon. You should prepare your excuses, Ham. Women don't like to be protected these days."

Ham paused and then glanced at Jack. He was far beyond pacing, standing in a deadly sort of stillness. The only movement was the twisting of his wedding ring around his finger. His voice was a bit of a croak as though he'd become a statue straight through the whole of his body.

"He said the back door wasn't locked," Jack said, finally answering Ham's question. "The shopgirl stated they tend to leave it open when deliveries arrive and they expected several more over the course of the day."

"You look like you're about to commit murder," Denny laughed nervously. "As if you're about to erupt into an act of violence."

"If I knew who to kill," Jack said quietly, "I would already be about it."

"Ah yes, well." Denny giggled. "If you need help burying a body, I'd suggest Smith. Not that I wouldn't help you, old man, but I suspect Smith might be a bit better at chucking a body without being caught."

Hargreaves cleared his throat from the doorway. "Sir, might I get you a bourbon?"

Jack didn't even respond for a long moment. "No."

"A sandwich?"

"No." Jack took a step away from the window. "Smith has

not responded to my telephone calls or messages. He had better have news."

"Where are the girls?" Denny asked.

"The babies were crying. They went up together," Victor replied. "They're probably rocking cradles and plotting nefarious things. Training up my daughters to be pretty devils. I have hopes that Agatha will be a bluestocking like her mother. Vivi, however, she's not even walking and she's pure trouble. May the good Lord bless me with a son."

Jack groaned, scrubbing his face with his hands. "Violet is going to do something rash. That's certain. She's too damned clever and brave for her own good. I have tried everything to find this man. It's like that brat prankster. You can't anticipate when they are going to strike. This fellow is too clever."

Victor hissed. "We're all staying here. Violet is safe enough. I am worried about you, old man. That X over your face was ominous."

"I'll be fine." Jack moved his wedding ring around his finger and faced the window, staring out. "Maybe whoever this fellow is, he's watching us now."

Ham chugged the rest of his cocktail. "What do you think? Was it that Jude Brown?"

Jack shrugged and Ham turned to Hargreaves.

"I don't know," the butler admitted. "I've seen people realize who Mrs. Vi is before. It was like that, sir. If the timing had been different, I wouldn't have been concerned, Mr. Wakefield."

Jack rubbed his brow. "He said something about Preston Bates. Perhaps that flower was not what he claimed. Perhaps the note was all just part of the act."

"We aren't going to know, yet," Ham said. "But we have something concrete now, don't we, with the park? I'm going to find the local bobby and see which of these houses around here have a few bachelors with bulldogs."

"I'll come with," Jack said.

"No," Ham snapped. "Victor, stay with Jack. Denny, use your bulk and tackle the man if he tries to leave."

"You aren't in charge here." Jack glared at his friend.

"I was your commander for a reason. I'm in charge of you at Scotland Yard for a reason," Ham told Jack. "I'm good at what I do, and you'll do better to not risk your self-control. Talk to Algie without Vi around. Find out what he can tell you about these fellows."

"Let's discuss from here," Victor told Jack, clapping him on the back. "Or I'll go with you to speak to Algie."

"Discuss what?" Jack hissed.

"We'll discuss what to do about these gents once we find them." Victor handed over his own cocktail with an expression that said Jack needed another drink to calm him down. When Victor turned back to the cocktail fixings, he barely hid his worry by making drinks.

"I know what to do," Jack said. "After all these cases, isn't it clear?"

"Jack!" Ham scolded. "We aren't going to murder someone. That's the easy way out, isn't it? We'll torture the fellow into giving up. Why just murder him when we can make him suffer."

Denny gasped and then giggled before he choked on the giggle so hard a tear slipped down his cheek. "I say, Victor, I have a new best friend now. It's Ham. He's got the vicious heart that I need to keep me true."

"Fine, fine," Victor said absently. "I've decided to replace you myself with Lila."

"Lila?" Denny breathed slowly. "Sold. You for Ham. You can have Lila. Violet will have to switch to Kate."

"Kate isn't wicked enough for Vi," Ham muttered. "It'll end up being Rita and then I'll be plagued by both you and Violet. No. We're staying put. Jack is my best friend. Victor is yours. Violet will keep Lila. Kate can be Rita's. Kate is an excellent choice for Rita."

"Enough of this," Jack snapped. "We'll all be each other's family and set aside the rankings. Now, tell me how to drive this man away from Violet."

"Perhaps Violet could simply drive the fellow away by being opposite of whatever he sees in her," Denny suggested. "I would take another cocktail, Victor. We all know my wits aren't up to anything worthwhile."

"The problem is that whatever this fiend sees in Vi isn't real." Jack glanced down at his drink and scowled, suddenly throwing it at the wall. The fragile cocktail glass shattered, but he didn't feel any better for the fit of temper. "They're obsessing over her as some sort of archetype. The witty earl's daughter who solves crimes and writes novels. The clever woman who has managed to keep her aunt's infamous investments producing."

"Mr. Wakefield, perhaps—" Hargreaves fell silent since there was nothing to offer.

Jack cursed low and then forced himself to continue. "This fellow doesn't know that she can't sleep half the time. That she finds her money a burden of doing good. She weighs her choices over what her Aunt Agatha would have done. Vi aches for what she didn't have with her mother. She's the most devoted aunt known to mankind. My God— she's haunted by the crimes against strangers. This fellow doesn't know any of that. She can't pretend to change to turn the man away. What he thinks he loves in her is mere foolish fancy."

~

VIOLET ROCKED baby Agatha while Vivi squalled at her mother.

"What are we going to do?" Kate asked as she walked back and forth bouncing Vivi.

"I don't know what to do." Lila glanced frantically among the two and then demanded. "Is she like this all the time?"

"She gets angry." Kate's mild tone had Lila gaping. "Vivi is an opinionated lass."

Violet frowned, rocking Agatha. "We have to find the man."

"How?" Kate asked before tutting to Vivi and adding a bounce to her walk.

"Algie and Clara must know where Preston lives," Lila suggested.

"I hardly think that Algie and Clara are the type to send out invites for their random parties. They just announce it's happening here and there and allow their rooms to be filled with strangers and friends." Violet fought to keep her anger out of her voice so Agatha didn't fly off the handle with her sister. She might be the sweeter of the twins, but she had a set of lungs on her that matched her sister.

Violet rose as Agatha relaxed against her and Vivi calmed down. "I'm going to the park."

"The park?" Kate asked, horrified.

"I'll be going out the back. I understand you have a gun. I'll be wanting it, just in case."

Kate shook her head. "Victor will kill me. You cannot go

alone, and I won't go with you."

Vi grinned and winked. "Lila will come."

"I will not." Lila rubbed her belly. "A mother protects her child."

Vi's gaze narrowed. "Victor would go with me, but he'll have been infected by Jack by now."

"Infected?" Kate asked, rocking the quieted Vivi.

"Jack is quite the manly, protective type," Lila answered. "He'll get that side of Victor wound up, and he'll forget all of Vi's training."

"Mmm," Violet agreed. "So busy protecting us, they don't think they might be in danger. There's no reason to think I might be hurt. It's Jack. Did you see that horrible X on his face?"

"I did," Kate said softly. "I—Vi, I don't know what I'd do if that were Victor. He loves me so dearly, and what a luxury that is."

"We're all quite spoiled that way," Vi said. "It's painful, really."

"You could get Denny to go with you," Lila suggested, taking the quieted Vivi from Kate. "He's more child than man, so he won't object, and he'll probably count on you protecting him instead of the other way round."

Violet bit her bottom lip around her wicked grin. "That would do. Denny is an excellent assistant for trouble until you two are back in fighting shape."

"Mrs. Kate," Nanny Jane said. "You need to have your tea and crackers, dear."

Violet rose. "I'll send one of the maids for the dogs and slip out the back. Lila, get me Denny. Kate, I need your gun." It said something about the unflappability of the nanny that she barely batted an eye at Violet's list of requests.

Violet took the servant's stairs down to the kitchen and found the cook. "Have you seen anyone about, Cook?" Vi took a biscuit from a platter.

"You mean anyone odd? Other than these odd fellows of Smith's?"

"Mmm," Vi agreed. "You see the deliveries coming and going through the kitchen. Anyone different?"

Cook shook her head. "Nothing different. The milkman, the baker delivery boy, the butcher's lad, they're all the same." She paused.

"But," Vi said, lifting a brow.

"But those boys might know something. They're regular enough to notice if things have been a bit odd. They deliver to more than just us, ma'am."

"When they deliver in the morning," Violet said as she took a second biscuit, "tell them if they come back at the end of their workday, I will reward them handsomely."

Vi clucked to her dogs and walked outside to find Denny waiting with a bit of a sick expression. "Your husband is a terrifying man."

"You'll be fine," Vi told him heartily, handing Denny the leash to Holmes. "Let's go out the walk between our house and Victor's house."

"Like we're hiding?" Denny's high-pitched squeak was enough to have Vi snorting. They were, of course, hiding their actions. "That will only give Jack a reason to strangle us."

"He'll never strangle *me*." Vi grinned over her shoulder and then slipped down the little pathway that had been created between her house and Victor's, bypassing the neighbor between their two houses. "It'll be fine, Denny. We're just trying to find out where they live."

CHAPTER 9

*V*iolet and Denny walked the park three times before they saw a daily maid with a bulldog. Vi grinned at Denny and then let Rouge off the leash. The friendlier of the two dogs would certainly dart towards a stranger dog. Vi followed after, calling an apology as the maid scooped up Rouge.

"Here you go, ma'am."

Vi took her dog, accepting the kiss on her chin as she squatted down to say hello to the bulldog. "Hello there, darling."

Vi scratched the dog's ears as Denny caught up.

"What a fine fellow he is," Denny said woodenly. He laughed a high-pitched squawk that had the maid eyeing him and taking a step back.

"Don't mind my friend," Violet said, standing. "He's never been right since the war. Your dog is so handsome."

"He's a right pain in my backside. Him and the rest of these bloody beasts. Too strong for me to take them all out, so he said just to take the one." The maid scowled down at the dog and then scoffed. "It's not my job to be walking dogs, but no one minds adding onto my burden and expecting me to work for the same tuppence. Refusing to take him out these days. Making me do it. Time for a new Wednesday position, that's for sure."

Vi gasped, holding her hand over her horrified mouth. She leaned in, a commiserating expression on her face. "They didn't!"

"They did," the maid snapped. "Cheap bastards."

"That is too cruel. Where do you work? Such fiends to add to your burdens. There's never enough time as it is for getting done what needs to be done."

The maid jerked her head to the south and then grunted. "I have to be going if I'm going to get the floors done. Come on, you ruddy great beast."

"You know," Violet said, "we can help. He does look like he pulls."

"He's pulling my arm out of the socket."

"Well, I can take our dogs," Violet told her lightly. "And Denny will take that one. We can see you back to your place of work. Tell me, is it a family you work for?"

"No," the maid said, shaking her head. "It would be easier to look after a slew of children. Instead, what I have is a couple who took the house from the owners. They've sublet the rooms to a whole slew of disgusting bachelors who are as likely to pinch as shove off their dogs on me."

Vi groaned. "Pinching men. They're the worst."

The maid eyed Denny and then lifted a brow at Denny.

"Oh don't worry about him. He's not a pincher."

Denny giggled and then leaned in and whispered low, "My wife has trained me very, very well. Also, Vi here."

"You're out with another woman and married?" The maid eyed the two of them. "Not my place. I'll let you take the dog, given I have to carry the mop bucket up and down the stairs and I'm already all wrenched up, but I don't approve of such things."

"Vi's my sister," Denny told the maid, leaving out all of the details. Siblings of the heart, perhaps might be the best way to describe. "Don't worry. I'm a bit of a rogue, perhaps, but I'm not that far gone."

They walked the maid across the park and realized that the house was nearly exactly across the park from Vi and Jack's house. The closer they got the more upset Violet became. Her stomach was roiling and she realized her hands were shaking again. Was it because of the anger that was riding her as though she were its horse? Or was it because of the way the house was just across from hers? She'd never once considered that her own house might be the avenue to why this fiend had targeted her.

The maid took the dog as they reached the other side of the park and thanked Denny. She was grumbling as she headed around the back of the house through a side gate. Denny tugged Violet away, but she only let him pull her as far as the next house and then they tucked into the area behind the next fence where they were mostly hidden from the house.

"Let's go tell the others we found the house," Denny said.

"Do you think the married couple is Roman Johnson and his wife?"

Denny sighed and then whispered low, "Vi! It's one thing to walk with you, and it's another to continue to get into trouble. Let's go back."

"I haven't said anything about getting into trouble."

"You don't have to. I've known you since we were in early days. That look in your eyes is the bedevil the people who care about you look."

"I don't have a look like that!"

"You do!" Denny groaned. "It's the same look you used when you pranked your stepmother. Just the same as when you first started talking about that pulp fiction you and Victor were publishing—knowing it would set off your family. The look on your face when you decided to learn how to drive. It's your trouble face, Mrs. Wakefield. Every time you get it on your face, poor Jack twitches."

Violet rubbed her brow and then shot Denny her best version of the trouble face and then looped Holmes and Rouge's leashes over the fence and then tiptoed down the side of the fence until they reached the back garden of the house. Vi could hear the bulldogs in the garden and then she grinned at Denny.

"No," he said.

"Bring Rouge and Holmes back here, so they'll be safe."

"No."

"Then open the gate, so the bulldogs go running."

"No, Vi. Bloody hell woman, what is your plan?"

Vi patted Denny's cheek. "You have gotten a bit plump, darling Denny. You had better climb the fence, pull the latch from this side. The dogs will catch you if you do it the other way round."

"Violet Wakefield, I am not doing any of this."

"If you don't help me," Vi said smoothly. "I'll just do it alone. What is worse, do you think?"

Denny groaned and then gasped as Violet took her dogs into the garden of the house. He followed after her mumbling, but when she opened the gate, closed it behind them, and then demanded his hand up, he shook his head strenuously. "They'll know we're here."

"Not if we're quiet. Especially with the bulldogs running wild in the street."

"Vi!"

"Denny, I am doing this. I am going to find out who this person is."

"Vi—" Denny was almost tearful. "Jack will kill me. And I'll be damned if I let anything happen to you. A man doesn't draw the kind of pictures that fellow drew of you if he doesn't have designs."

"Or the X over Jack's face. If he doesn't see Jack as an obstacle."

"It's a man's job," Denny shot back, "to protect his wife and family."

"Jack knew what he was getting when he married me."

Denny stared at her open-mouthed and then to her surprise, he laughed. "He did."

"It's his fault," Violet said with a wicked grin.

"Entirely. You'll protect me, won't you?"

"I will." They glanced at each other, each knowing that Jack would be tempted, at the least, to strangle both of them.

"I'm a big fan of your husband, did you know? Never wanted you to marry Tomas even though he's my friend."

"I'd have driven Tomas mad."

"In days." Denny laughed again and cupped his hands, lifting her until she could open the gate.

She held out her hand leaning over the fence and ignoring the way it dug into her ribs. "Hand me Holmes's ball."

Denny handed it over and she whistled. The dogs came running, including the massive beast who had been too much for the maid. Vi cooed to them and waved the ball back and forth. The moment that their gazes fixed on the ball, she threw it as hard as she could and then reached out to close the gate, so they couldn't get back in.

With Denny still holding her high, Violet put her hands down and then pulled herself over the fence, dropping on the other side. Her dogs whined and Violet whispered, "Quiet."

Their whining lowered to a nearly inaudible objection at being separated from her. Violet whispered, "I'll be back, my darlings."

Denny struggled to the top of the gate; his face was red with the struggle and he couldn't quite pull himself over. "Never tell anyone."

"Never," Violet laughed, reaching up to pull on him and giving him the edge that pulled him over the fence and had him tumbling to the ground.

Violet took a deep breath in and then held out her hands giving Denny a haul up.

He groaned with a low tone. "Lila might be right about me needing to be a little more active."

"Perhaps a smidgeon," Violet whispered back. Their gazes met and they crept across the grass towards the back windows. Violet pressed up on her toes and peeked into the first window and then dropped to her knees.

"Someone there?" Denny asked on his knees next to her. "What do we do?"

"We are going to find our way to a door, let ourselves in, and search the house."

"Vi! It's occupied! They'll find us. Maybe your fellow will find us."

"He's not mine," Vi said, elbowing Denny hard.

He gasped against the pain and then muttered a low apology. She crawled until they were below another window and then she slowly pushed herself to her toes. "This one is empty."

There was a shout inside of the house and the slamming of a door.

"They've discovered the dogs." Vi checked the window and discovered it unlocked. She pushed it open and then told Denny. "Help me in."

"We're going to get caught."

"I'll pay your fines."

Denny groaned and then put his hands on her waist, lifting her inside of the house. The window was lower than the gate, so he was able to pull himself in much easier. Vi grinned at him, noting the mud on his knees.

"We're going to be committed if we're caught like this."

Vi winked at him and glanced around. It was simply a small office with a desk. Slowly, she opened the desk drawer and flipped through the contents of the desk. The terrible handwriting was quite the opposite of the neat blocky letters in the notes she had received.

She slowly closed the drawers of the desk and joined Denny on the wall near the door. She dared to twist the handle of the door and peek out through the crack. "The hall is clear."

"So?"

"Let's check the bedrooms."

"Bloody hell, Vi," Denny moaned.

She slipped out the door and hurried down the hall. There was a servant's hall at the end, and Violet darted up the steps.

"We're going to get caught."

"Roman Johnson and the rest aren't wealthy enough to

have regular servants." Vi wasn't even trying to hide herself anymore.

"What? Quiet!"

Violet shook her head at Denny. "They're sharing the rental of this place. Their wealth is a sham, Denny. They don't have regular servants. They have a daily maid who comes only on Wednesdays."

Denny stared at her and then looked at the stairs. "These are a bit dusty."

"They have regular stairs to use. The servant's stairs will get us where we need to be without being seen." Vi said, nodding.

"What about the maid?"

"She has no loyalty to them, and I have money in my pocket."

Denny paused and then his head tilted before he nodded. They finished making their way up the steps. They reached the second floor and Denny refused to let Vi open the doors. He did instead.

"There's no one there."

They left the stairs and closed the servant's door. Just as they did, there was the sound of someone coming up the front staircase. Their gazes met in panic and Denny darted across the hall, opened the first bedroom door, and yanked Vi in behind him.

Denny closed the bedroom door just, and they both collapsed against it just as they realized that they'd almost been caught.

"It could have been the maid," Denny said with a low, tortured whisper.

"She's certainly cleaning the common areas."

"Then who?"

Vi shook her head, but they both knew that they could easily be caught. "Someone who lives here, probably."

A moment later there was a sound at the door and Denny gasped. Vi put her hand over his face and tugged him towards the dark corner behind the oversized armoire. As the door opened, Denny's wide panicked gaze met Vi's.

"We'll be fine," she mouthed.

The door closed behind and they could hear the precise clip of a step.

CHAPTER 10

"Jack," Ham said, "will at least consider murdering you both. He might murder you, Denny. And if he were a man to lay hands on a woman—"

"I wouldn't have married him. How did you know we were here?"

"I found the local bobby and had him show me the house. Then I followed him here only to see a pack of bulldogs running amuck. A closed back gate. Two of the sweetest dogs known to mankind quietly whining for their mistress."

"Did you leave them?"

"I sent your dogs home with the local bobby and let myself into the house. The owners are chasing their dogs down the street. We've only so much time."

Vi laughed and kissed Ham's cheek. "Let's do this."

Vi turned back to the bedroom. "The maid was right. These bachelors are disgusting."

The room was covered with laundry. There was evidence

that the fellow had been eating in his room for days and the dishes were encrusted with flies hovering. Violet gagged and then patted Denny on the arm.

"You take this one. Bring a sample of his writing. We'll see if the person who wrote those letters lives in this house."

Violet darted to the next bedroom. It was neat as a pin with military tight corners on the bed, an armoire full of suits, and not a single example of writing. She sighed and then saw Ham in the next room. She was tempted to follow him, but a thought struck her. Those stairs had kept going up. Vi considered again following Ham, but he would search thoroughly. Better than her. It was probably just an attic. It was probably just storage boxes, but it would bother her if she didn't at least check.

Violet went back to the servants' steps and followed them up. She found empty servants' bedrooms and then followed it a little higher and found that the attic had been turned nursery. There were old, small beds and a cradle that had been covered in a sheet. A dollhouse, mostly garbage, had been left in the corner and not far was a rocking horse that was missing one of the rockers, the tail, and both eyes.

Violet's gaze moved all of those things without pausing and then she stared in horror at the opposite side of the room. Most of the windows had been left dirty, but a whole row on the side of the house that faced the park had been cleaned until they shone.

There was an easel near the windows and a whole stack of papers. Violet crossed to them and found, to her horror, drawing after drawing of herself. There were many, *many*, where she wasn't wearing clothes. Vi grabbed the whole lot, with little care that someone would know she'd been there.

She glanced at the windows again and realized that there was a spyglass sitting on the windowsill.

She gasped and then picked it up. Whoever was using it would only be able to see her front door, but perhaps that was why the flowers arrived when she wasn't there, why the notes and little messages, why they might have been able to find her after she'd randomly gone shopping. It wasn't as if she had a schedule for when she might go.

She slammed it down, breaking it after the third bash. The glass shattered out of the metal tube. She bit down on her bottom lip and then looked out the window. Her house was so easily seen from this vantage point. She glanced down and noticed two gentlemen approaching with bulldogs held by the collar.

Vi gasped, clutching the drawings to her chest and spun for the stairs. She darted down them and then hissed, "Ham! Denny! They're back."

Ham appeared, grabbing Denny by the arm, and rushed towards the servants' stairs.

Ham's gaze fixed on the contents of Vi's bundle. "Is that what I think it is?"

Vi didn't answer, but she guessed her expression or pallor was all he needed for an affirmative. Ham's face turned hard and he opened the back door just as the front door opened. They ran towards the gate and darted around to the next garden as the back door opened and the bulldogs were released. The dogs immediately caught the scent of them and they ran at the gate, jumping at it until it shook.

"We're going to be mauled by those dogs," Denny whispered.

"Nonsense," Violet whispered back. "Just you, Denny. Ham and I can certainly outrun you."

Denny gasped and Ham said, "This way. We'll let ourselves out the other side and hope we aren't witnessed."

Violet would have followed, but Ham pushed her ahead of him.

"They aren't going to shoot, Vi," Denny complained. "Protect me instead."

"Just get moving! I could lose my position for this."

"Why don't you?" Denny asked. "Marry Rita. Help her father look after her money."

"I don't want my mind to rot like yours," Ham said dryly.

The sarcasm was likely what prompted Denny's reply. "Then perhaps Smith would hire you."

Vi gasped and choked on a laugh since she was trying to be silent. Ham rushed them both along and made them circle round the street and come upon their house on the opposite side. Vi had a moment of sheer hatred for her house, but she refused to let it linger. She loved the house she and Jack had bought and redone together. She loved how close it was to the house that Victor and Kate owned—even if they were staying with Violet and Jack during this visit.

She loved the massive back garden and the mistress's bedroom that had become a private lounge for herself since she and Jack shared the master room. She loved the house and everything about it and whoever was focused on her was not going to ruin those feelings.

AFTER THEY'D CHANGED from crawling through the flowerbeds, Denny cleared his throat. "So, who's going to tell Jack?"

"Not I," Ham said flatly. "I might have joined you two in

that foolishness, but I would never have brought Violet along."

"Oh do stuff it," Violet muttered, calling to her brother, "Victor I need a cocktail!"

"Vi—" He sniffed delicately. "Jack is a bit terrifying, you know. We can't pull the wool over his gaze. He'll find us out."

"I will tell him," Violet said. She looked at the pile of drawings again. She hadn't let anyone else pick them up or look at them. "Did we find any handwriting samples?"

Ham shook his head. "We have what we need, Vi. Now we just need time. You *do* need to be the one to tell Jack."

"I have said I would." Vi rolled her eyes.

"Tell me what?" His voice was a cold fury.

Vi glanced at Jack. Behind him was her cousin Algie, who giggled nervously echoed by Denny.

"We snuck into the bulldog house."

"You did what?" He didn't even sound surprised. "I suppose you found something."

Vi's gaze darted to the drawing, but she didn't point them out. Jack's tightening jaw showed he saw them and recognized what they were.

"Who is it then?"

"We don't know," Ham muttered. "It's lived in by Roman and Heather Johnson. They've sublet four bedrooms to bachelors that we haven't identified yet."

Vi took a deep breath in.

"They'll know we've discovered them." Jack lifted the stack of drawings of Violet and crossed to the door, leaving the parlor and walking down the hall to the library. He was followed by everyone as if he were the pied piper. Violet, Ham, Victor, and Denny.

Jack opened the safe and shoved the drawings in, slamming it closed. "I need a drink."

"How long will it take before we have a reaction?" Denny asked. "I—well, I'm sorry. I just thought we were walking in the park."

Jack snorted. "You knew better."

"He tried," Violet told Jack.

His gaze landed on her, and she could see the anger. He almost pulsated with it, but Violet had little fear. She waited while Victor poured Jack a stiff bourbon and then handed glasses all round.

"What happened?" Jack asked, slumping into a seat.

Violet recapped the events and then said, "I'm not sorry."

Ham cleared his throat and grabbed Denny by the back of his jacket, hauling him, protesting, from the library. They were followed by Victor who left Jack with the advice, "Wringing her neck will leave you ultimately unhappy."

Jack eyed Violet who met his gaze without fear. He finally said, "You aren't sorry."

She shook her head and then sipped from her glass, wincing at the burn. With all of the stress of the day, her stomach didn't happily accept the strong alcohol on top of the afternoon.

"Ham warned me that you'd do something rash."

Violet lifted a brow.

"I knew you would. Since Ham had taken the house, I thought I'd sneak out and handle Algie."

"Stupid." She had little sympathy.

"Indeed." He opened his arms, and Violet settled on his lap, pouring the rest of her drink into his glass. "Victor should have known you'd want ginger wine."

Violet shook her head. She didn't care about the wine or

the bourbon. "Why is this happening? It's not like I did anything. When I go to the park—"

"It's not your fault, Violet." His hand rubbed her back and he sighed. "Even if you were prancing through the park naked, it's not your fault."

"He seems to think that you're in the way." Violet tangled their fingers together. "I won't have that. You promised me a lifetime of happiness."

"I did promise that." Jack turned their tangled hands towards him and placed a kiss on the back of them.

"What did Algie say?"

"He's known them for quite a long time, but they were never very good friends. They go to each other's parties, run into each other at the races, buy each other drinks if they happen to meet at the club. And then they never think of each other again."

Violet's mouth twisted. "How do we find which one of them it is?"

"It won't take long," Jack told her as he pressed a kiss against her forehead. "Our suspects just went from the whole of London to the residents of one house that we don't even have to leave ours to watch."

"Once he replaces his spy glass," Vi said with a shudder, "I'm afraid the same may be true of him."

Jack snorted. "I have some ideas on that front. I am going to make an appointment with your man of business and hire overt guards now. We'll have the same fellows inside of our house."

"He must know who they are," Vi said, pulling back to watch Jack's face. "He's been watching our house. All of the sudden we have three additional men into our house?"

"I've armed Hargreaves and a few of the other servants as well."

"It won't come to that," Violet said fiercely. "We're going to win this without having to pull weapons and defend our home."

CHAPTER 11

*S*mith entered the house without knocking and helped himself to a drink before Violet had reached the parlor to request afternoon tea be brought in. It had been a day since Jack had left Violet in the library and disappeared for hours with Ham. Violet hoped that whatever illegal things had been done were perpetrated by Smith instead of Jack, but she had little doubt that whatever had been done was what brought Smith to her house in the middle of the afternoon.

"I object to you giving Beatrice time off," he said without any further greeting.

"Her cousin was getting married."

"So?" Smith lifted one of his perfect brows over his perfect eyes and gave Violet a daggered glance. "They don't appreciate her as they should."

Vi laughed and then bypassed him to make her way to the bar cart. The coffee and tea were coming, and she'd put in a special request for strawberry scones, but Vi thought that ginger wine would be a better choice. The events of the last few weeks demanded something more than lapsang souchong or even Turkish coffee.

"How do you know that they don't appreciate her?"

"They don't write her enough. They object that you took her away and that they don't see her, so they punish her with a lack of news."

Violet very much doubted his assessment, but she also suspected that Smith knew very little about functioning families, let alone families that loved each other. "Are you writing to her while she's there?"

"No," Smith snorted. "Do I look like a pansy?"

No, Violet thought, he looked like an angel until you noticed his eyes. They were pure devil. He was as aware of his surroundings as Jack or Ham, but there was something that declared Smith was weighing mankind and finding them wanting. Let alone the surety that he was plotting a hundred different crimes all while he flashed that sardonic smile.

"Don't you want her thinking of you?" Violet had only seen Smith seem human when Beatrice, Violet's business manager, was present.

"I'm unforgettable." His smooth smile made Violet reassess her guess that he'd abandoned Beatrice to her family. Vi would bet a good amount of money that he was doing something to keep himself in Beatrice's thoughts. Probably something that left Beatrice blushing and stammering.

"You miss her."

"She's one in a million."

Smith glanced Violet over, and she felt that he was certainly seeing more than she wanted him to. Could he tell how her soul was at civil war? Both afraid and mocking herself for being so up in arms about a few drawings? Could he tell how she felt as though she were being hunted, how her skin didn't seem to fit right anymore? How she felt as though eyes were on her even when she knew they weren't? Could he see how she took a long bath with a towel over her body? Could he tell how she'd curled so tightly into Jack's body the night before that an intruder would have had trouble realizing she was in the bed as well?

"I do like her," Violet said lamely, shivering as her thoughts assaulted her.

"You know, your man might obsess over you like I obsess over Beatrice."

"Oddly," Violet told him, wondering if she was comforting the man, "Beatrice doesn't object to your attentions."

Smith scoffed and then made himself a second drink. "May I see the drawings he made of you?"

"No," Violet snapped. "He has a penchant for drawing me without clothes."

"But he hasn't seen you naked. The other side of the park looks at the front of the house. Your rooms with Jack over-look the garden. That isn't your body. It's his fantasy of your body."

"It's my face."

"I'm sure you're more flawed than whatever he's drawing."

Violet stared at Smith, taking in his evil smirk. She winced and then admitted, "There is little comfort in that."

"Do you want me to kill him?"

Vi stared. The question had been so utterly casual that he sounded as if he was asking if she wanted her wine topped off. Violet started to say no, but a part of her heart was demanding that she say yes. She stared at him, gaping, until his cold laugh snapped her back to herself.

"Part of you wants to say yes." Smith sounded so completely satisfied that Violet wanted to deny it, but it was the truth. A very large part of herself wanted to say yes.

"Maybe." That was a lie, and Smith's expression said he knew it.

"Where are your lines?"

She started to say that murder was the other side of the line, but to her surprise it wasn't. "Don't let Jack kill him."

Smith 's mouth twisted, but there was the glint of approval in his gaze as he nodded. "I don't like anyone but Beatrice, but you and Jack are the closest it gets for me. Beatrice, however, adores you."

Vi bit her bottom lip, but she wasn't hiding anything when she replied, "I adore her back, and I'll take your help even if you only give it because you love her."

He snorted. "I'll be charging you as well."

"I don't care about the money. I'll do whatever it takes to keep my family safe."

Smith started to reply but closed his mouth as Denny came into the room, followed by Lila who somehow seemed to glow and be exhausted at the same time.

"Ah," Lila yawned prettily and then winked at Smith, "my favorite villain."

He lifted a brow and then said, "My favorite useless housewife."

Lila saluted Smith and demanded a cocktail. Victor and Kate, each with a baby in arms, entered next and Victor handed Denny baby Vivi and crossed to the bar, taking up his role of making drinks.

"Where's Ham?" Violet asked as Jack entered. He had the look that said he'd stayed up all night to watch over her, but she knew he'd never left her side. She had been restless to the extent he'd had to throw an arm and leg over her and help her settle down.

"Rita arrived on the night train. Ham took her to the hotel to get some sleep and is bringing her."

Vi lifted both brows. That wasn't like Rita at all. Leaving Kate's mother at night? Very odd. The frisson of awareness that something was amiss moved through the group of friends. "She should stay with us."

Jack nodded absently. She could feel his gaze moving over her, lingering on the jumper that covered her from her neck to her wrist and long past her waist. His gaze went back to her face and she was sure he noticed the dark circles under her eyes or the way she was avoiding his gaze. She didn't want him to worry, and she knew he'd notice that haunted look in her eyes.

After too long of avoiding his gaze, she turned her eyes to his. She didn't like trying to hide herself from him. Instead, she let him see the worry and the fear.

"It rather feels like someone has let loose wild animals in the park, doesn't it?" Denny asked. "Found myself going out with the servants to take out the dogs."

"The girls slept in our room last night," Kate admitted. "I don't like the way those drawings make me feel."

"It's like a lion is stalking our home," Victor agreed. "I got up twice to check the locks of the windows and doors even though I knew that Hargreaves and Jack had done the same."

"As did I," Denny admitted. "Then I worried that I messed it up and double checked them again."

"From the sounds of it," Smith said, "you basically had a

watch running. You should just coordinate next time. Save my men a bit of work and sleep given that they were watching the house as well."

"We'll keep up the double layer," Jack said evenly. "I'd rather we overprotect than under. No mistakes. No weaknesses if we can avoid it. We don't know what kind of man we're dealing with. Is he just going to harass from afar? Is he someone we can scare off? Is he a madman who will lock the doors and light the house on fire?"

"Oh my," Kate said, blinking rapidly. "That escalated rather quickly for me."

Her gaze darted around the room, but it lingered on her daughters.

"Don't worry," Smith told them. "The local bobby is a rather effective fellow and he's got an extra man on the job. One just to keep an eye on your place. When you add in the cretins who I hired and the attention inside the house, the fellow isn't going to breach the house, and your daughters will be fine."

"If I wanted to get Vi," Denny said, "my attention would be on the girls."

They all shot him horrified looks and Denny held out his hands in surrender, but he wasn't wrong, and all of them knew it.

"The babies, Jack, Victor. The rest of us. We're Vi's weaknesses," Kate said. "There isn't anything that Vi wouldn't do for us."

"This fellow isn't going to know that," Jack said. "This has started relatively recently as far as we know. If we base it off when he started making himself known—and they've only lived in that house since December—then the twins have never been here. He has no idea about what makes Vi really tick."

Denny glanced at Vi and then said, "We should gather up the articles that have been written about you and the books you write. That must be what he's pulling from. That and—perhaps—memories."

"Denny old boy," Victor said with an air of surprise, "that was helpful."

Lila snorted as the door to the parlor opened and Rita and Ham entered. Everyone jumped to their feet, surrounding Rita with greetings. By the time they'd quieted, the tea had arrived. Cook had gone wild with trays of scones, sandwiches, cakes, biscuits, and little nibbles. The teapot and coffee pot were full and there was food for everyone.

They gathered around the cart and then as they started to eat, Hargreaves appeared again with one of Smith's men and two chalkboards being rolled into the parlor.

"Denny—" Jack groaned.

"We need to collate information," Denny said imperiously. "Write down what we know about these folks and start ruling them out. We all know this method works."

Violet took a bite of her strawberry scone and chased the bite with an oversized sip of her ginger wine. She leaned back and sighed.

"Ham," Violet asked suddenly. "What about the cases you've seen that happen like this? What happens?"

"Nothing," Smith told Violet. "These fellows don't break any laws or leave any clues until it's too late."

"Too late?" Lila asked. "That sounds like it ends with murder."

"Murder. Other things." Smith's vague reference was dark enough that they all shivered.

"How does it end?" Rita demanded of Ham, making him focus on her.

"It ends with death, kidnapping, and rape. This kind of long slow hunt is meant to avoid the lines that the laws put in place to protect society."

"But that's not right—" Kate muttered. Her gaze returned to her daughters again.

"Sometimes the victim just disappears and we don't know what happened. Did she flee? Or did he get her?"

Rita cleared her throat and her large blue eyes moved among the friends.

"What?" Ham asked her.

Kate stared and then slowly said, "There was the story of a girl."

Rita nodded. "Your mother said she didn't tell you all of it."

"What do you mean?" Kate asked.

Rita had taken them all captive with her words, and Violet felt a sense of horror.

Rita fiddled her with her teacup as she said hoarsely, "Your mother didn't know all of it. What she knew was that there was a tale of Roman and his friends driving some girl mad. She disappeared. No one knows what happened to her."

CHAPTER 12

"*A*s a group?" Jack demanded, thrusting himself to his feet and crossing to Vi's chair as though proximity would save her from whatever had happened thus far. "They drove this girl mad as a group?"

Rita shrugged and then admitted, "Mrs. Lancaster didn't know for sure. She only knew the rumors. At least one of the friends pursued a girl from a small town and then she was suddenly gone. She's going to try to find out the name of the girl and where it was. She'll telegram if she can."

Smith rose, setting aside his cocktail, and crossed to the chalkboards. He wrote with neat handwriting on the board.

ROMAN JOHNSON
    HEATHER JOHNSON
    BARNABY GALLAGHER
    PRESTON BATES
    JUDE BROWN
    MARVIN WASHINGTON

To the group, Smith said, "The house is leased to the very elderly aunt of Heather Johnson. Given what I was able to discover in the time I've had so far, I think that Aunt Maude may have no idea of the day of the week let alone how things have been leased."

"Lovely," Rita said low.

"They have sublet rooms to the gents on this list. I don't like any of them, but I don't generally care for the human race."

Smith gestured to the first name of the gents renting. "Barnaby Gallagher works for the law offices of Seal, Seal, and Janes. He's a low level lawyer there and isn't particularly well liked by anyone who works with him."

"No rising star, our Barnaby?" Denny asked. "Not a surprise if he's our man."

"It could be any of them in that house," Jack muttered. "Smith did you search the house?"

"I did," Smith agreed. "There's nothing incriminating beyond the broken spyglass in the attic and the empty easel. Vi won't let me see the drawings."

"That goes for all of us," Denny told Smith. "You don't want Jack to feel the need to worry you."

"What drawings?" Rita demanded. "What has happened?"

Ham leaned close, whispering in Rita's ear the backstory while Violet crossed to stand next to Smith at the chalk-boards. While Ham explained, Vi wrote on the chalkboard.

ROMAN JOHNSON — married to Heather Johnson. It was Heather that was known by Kate's mother. Possibly involved in some sort of previous incident where the victim disappeared. Nefarious enough to take advantage of an elderly woman and use her finances to secure a house that he can't afford.

HEATHER JOHNSON — married to Roman. Her family is the ones who spread the rumors about this group of friends. She is somehow connected to a previous stalker of women. Does she know the nature of those she associates with?

BARNABY GALLAGHER — Works as a lawyer. Isn't well liked.

"WHAT ABOUT PRESTON BATES?" Violet asked. "What did you learn about him?"

Smith lifted a brow and then said, "He's currently unemployed. He's worked here and there, but he has enough money to avoid working. A gift from a grandparent combined with a windfall from gambling if my research is correct."

"Who was the windfall from?" Vi demanded.

"Theodophilus Smythe-Hill. Evidence suggests that Preston Bates allowed that Smythe fellow to attempt a trap and the hunter became the hunted."

"Really?" Denny's shout of laughter was emphasized by slapping his hand on his leg. "I wonder if he was just lucky or if he really did twist events on Theo."

"Evidence also suggests that Theo won his money from Algie, whose debts were paid by your Aunt Agatha. Given that you were the major inheritor, Vi, it could be said that you are the one who is supporting Preston in his lifestyle."

Vi stared at Smith who smiled back, enjoying her horror.

She shook off her reaction. "If that was purposeful, he's already shown he was a hunter."

"Indeed," Smith agreed. "I thought that was interesting as well."

Violet wrote under his name on the board.

PRESTON BATES — Lives off of a small inheritance and gambling winnings. Associated with a group of friends who already drove one woman into ____ (Where did she go) (Is she still alive?) Was Preston the reason that happened? Did he create himself a fortune by manipulating a monster? Or was it luck? Perhaps Preston intended to punish Theo?

Vi scowled at the name. All of the hairs on the back of her neck were crawling, and Vi could have easily said that it seemed someone had walked over her grave. She fiddled with her wedding ring.

"Mylo Hunt is not on here."

"He has a flat in Chelsea," Smith told Violet. "He spends rather a lot of time with these folks, particularly Barnaby, but he doesn't live in that house. He also works as a banker and is quite well-liked in his office."

"He's a jerk and a fiend." Vi glanced at Jack and then shrugged. "I didn't like how he responded to Jack."

"Well," Smith said, "not all of us like Scotland Yard men, myself included."

"You almost like Jack though," Vi shot back. "So that's not saying much."

"His brother was killed in a riot," Smith said. "To all accounts the police officers made it worse."

"Well now," Victor inserted, "I'd hold a grudge on that one myself."

"Just because there was one bad police officer doesn't mean that we're all responsible," Ham snapped.

"But you won't be working for Scotland Yard long will you?" Denny giggled and then said to Smith, "It's been suggested that you might like to take on Jack and Ham as apprentices."

Rita gasped and then covered her mouth to hold back the giggles while Lila simply raised her drink.

"Oh my," Kate said.

"Hell no," Ham replied. "I have standards."

"As do I," Smith snapped. "You two lumbering maidens would be useless for real work."

"Well now," Victor said, shoving another glass in Smith's hand. "Let's all be friendly here."

"We need people like Smith," Vi said precisely. "He can do what Ham and Jack cannot."

"And," Rita added, "we need Ham and Jack who can bring down the arm of justice."

"And right now," Jack added evenly, "we're far more benefited by someone of Smith's skillset than either of ours. Thank you, Smith. I mean that."

"Ahhh," Denny cooed. "we've another bird in the nest. Welcome to the family, Smith. We're a plaguesome crew."

"I've noticed," Smith said dryly. "Jude Brown is Preston Bate's cousin. They were raised in the same house, received the same inheritance, and somehow Jude has never needed to work. He took firsts in mathematics at Oxford, his bedroom is crowded with novels, including the V.V. Twinnings books, and he seems to be something of a bookworm and bluestocking."

"That's a term for girls, old boy," Denny said.

"Well." Smith smiled evilly. "Any one of our girls could

outman him any day. Feels like a more feminine term would be just the thing."

Denny snorted and Vi shook her head. Reexamining the list of residents of that house and the last named, Marvin Washington. Was it possible that the person was the one? Someone she had never met? Someone she had never seen? She could pass him on the street and not realize who she was facing.

"What about this man?" Vi asked, cutting into the back and forth between Smith and Denny. "Marvin Washington? Who is that?"

"Works with Mylo Hunt. Has a lady named Gayle Cline. He also had a disgusting set of rooms along with some debts and IOUs and rather a ridiculous personal collection of gin, rum, and wine where his clothes should have been."

Vi frowned. He seemed rather innocuous really.

"Perhaps he has to hide his things in his rooms because his roommates cannot be trusted." Kate glanced at the others and then rose to walk the fussy Agatha. "None of them seem like someone you could trust around your open handbag."

"What I want to know," Rita added, "is whether he was there when the previous girl disappeared."

"That does seem to be a key point. We must find out more about that." Jack rubbed the back of his neck, and Vi could feel his gaze land on her as he said, "Surely whoever was behind that is behind this for Violet."

She shook her head and examined the board, making notes as she worked on it until it read:

ROMAN JOHNSON — married to Heather Johnson. It was Heather that was known by Kate's mother. Possibly involved in some sort of previous incident where the victim disappeared. Nefarious enough to take advantage of an elderly woman and use her finances to secure a house that he can't afford.

HEATHER JOHNSON — married to Roman. Her family are the ones who spread the rumors about this group of friends. She is somehow connected to a previous stalker of women. Does she know the nature of those she associates with? Is she aware of her aunt's financial situation being used for the house?

BARNABY GALLAGHER — Works as a lawyer. Isn't well liked at his office. Surely whoever is leaving all of this stuff and stealing Vi's things and drawing those pictures wouldn't be well liked?

PRESTON BATES — Lives off of a small inheritance and gambling winnings. Associated with a group of friends who already drove one woman into ____ (Where did she go) (Is she still alive?) Was Preston the reason that happened? Did he create himself a fortune by manipulating a monster? Or was it luck? Perhaps Preston intended to punish Theo?

JUDE BROWN — Lives in the house as well. Appeared at the bookstore directly after Violet's underthings were stolen. He seems to know rather a lot about Vi through her books. He doesn't work and he is quite clever. A first in mathematics is nothing to discount. Something of an intellectual. Why doesn't he have to work? Does he have some other inheritance?

MARVIN WASHINGTON — Has a job and a lady friend. Does that lady friend disqualify him from being the one pursuing Violet? Has some debts and doesn't spend as much time with the other residents. Perhaps the least likely of the residents to be the one watching Vi.

THOUGHTS:

The flowers and jewelry have not been low-cost things. Would any member of the house have the money to do those things? Where does that money come from?

How did Vi come to the attention of this fellow? What is it in her that makes him obsessed?

What happened to the other woman? She disappeared. Did she run? Is she dead?

Rita rose and stood next to Violet, reading the board over until Rita turned to face Vi. "Whatever happened to that woman is not going to happen to you, Vi."

Vi tried to smile, but she couldn't quite. The memory of that spyglass in her hands, the stack of drawings that showed she'd gained someone's attention to the exclusion of all else. How was she supposed to defend against that? How was she supposed to prevent being the object of this kind of obsession when she had no idea of what she had done to gain this attention.

"Let's go dancing," Violet said after they stepped away from the chalkboard and turned back to the sandwiches and scones. "Rita is back. We should welcome her properly. Dinner somewhere fabulous. Dancing. Cocktails."

"She probably just wants Indian food," Ham said. "She has been sick of roast meals and fish for weeks."

"I do want Indian food," Rita said. "I want that paneer stuff with the red sauce. And naan. And samosas. And a lassi."

"That all sounds fabulous," Violet agreed, "Dinner, cocktails, *dancing.*"

Almost as one, everyone's gaze moved to Jack. "We don't know what happened to that other girl. Until we do, we assume it was the worst and we act accordingly. Keep each other in sight and let's make a dramatic exit. We'll see who follows."

Vi grinned. "I have just the dress."

CHAPTER 13

*V*iolet and Rita dressed together as Rita's clothes were at the hotel and Ham preferred them to stay together. Vi glanced through her dresses. Rita was both taller and more voluptuous, but they weren't so far different in size that it was impossible to share.

Violet dug through her dresses until she found one that had no back and buttoned around the neck. It showed a bit more of Rita's sides than it did on Vi, but it would do. The dress was a brilliant blue and it made Rita's eyes seem twice as large. With red lipstick, she was utterly dashing.

"I can't compete. You're going to steal my unwanted admirer and Ham will be the one debating murder."

Violet grinned at the alarmed expression on Rita's face and then dug through her jewelry until she found a sapphire choker, sapphire earbobs, and a long strand of cream pearls. There was no way for Rita to wear Violet's shoes, but Kate was much taller, and her shoes would work. Rita left to find shoes with Kate while Violet dug through her closet.

Vi considered a black dress for a long moment and then moved it aside for a short silver dress. The fringe would reach past her knees, but the fabric itself didn't. With her black pearls and a diamond choker, she'd simply glisten.

Violet put on her underthings, her stockings, and then dropped the dress over her head. A moment later there was a knock at the door and Jack entered.

"Vi?"

She glanced up from latching her diamond t-strap shoes.

"I need you to stay with someone the whole time we're there."

"Jack, darling," Violet said with a laugh as she patted his cheek, "I have no desire to be kidnapped, murdered, or assaulted. Perhaps this fellow just wants to talk, but if he were a normal man, he'd approach in the park and said hello and I'd have waxed poetic about my husband."

"Poetic."

Vi turned back to her mirror, glancing over her shoulder at him as she repeated, "Poetic." She started to quote some poem and came up dry. "Ok, I can't deliver. But I would if I weren't distracted."

Jack leaned down and kissed her forehead. "I don't need a poem, Vi darling. I just need you to be safe."

"Promise," Vi swore, linking their pinkies together.

Jack leaned down, setting his chin on top of her head. "I'll hold you to it. Now hurry up. Those sandwiches did nothing for me after Rita started talking about samosas."

Vi winked at him, put on her jewelry, and left him to change his suit into something more dapper.

∼

JACK REQUESTED Hargreaves to bring the autos around early and leave them in the front of the house, so their exit would be obvious. The autos sat outside for a good forty-five minutes until the first auto left. Containing Rita, Ham, Denny and Lila, the auto left a while earlier and there was a black cab waiting with one of Smith's men to follow and see if the first auto was followed.

Vi's auto left several minutes later and Jack sat in the front, so he could have reason to turn around. To an observer, it would seem like he was simply talking with the occupants of the backseat. For Jack's purposes, however, he was watching to see if they were followed.

"What do you think?" Victor asked. "Will we have visitors on our next endeavor?"

Victor didn't turn around to see and Jack didn't answer, but they could all tell by the flexing of Jack's jaw that they were being followed. Their auto stopped outside of the Indian restaurant and as they piled inside, they found their friends had already secured a table and ordered a mountain of food. Vi sidled in next to Rita and whispered, "Were you followed?"

Rita shook her head. "You?"

Vi's gaze jerked towards the door and while they watched, they found Roman Johnson and Heather Johnson enter, followed by all of their roommates except the one Violet hadn't met yet. She glanced at Jack as he dramatically laid his arm over the back of her chair. His eyes glinted a little, and Violet snorted. He pressed a kiss on her forehead and then leaned down to lay a very soft kiss on her lips.

"Do you want to put your name on me? Somewhere conspicuous?" she whispered.

His grin wasn't forced when he tapped her forehead and

then pressed another kiss just where her finger had been resting.

"Did I hear you offering to wear a label?" Denny asked. "Because, if so, may I suggest—Devilish."

"Or perhaps instigator?" Ham replied. "Rita would have been well kept out of this business."

"I would suggest friends with foolish men," Rita replied dryly. "You had best be careful, my love." Her gaze was steely. "I don't want a caretaker; I want a partner."

Violet huffed a low laugh, raising her mango lassi to Rita.

"Are we celebrating?" a voice asked and Vi's whole table turned as one. It was as though blood was in the water and a school of piranhas had just caught the scent.

"We are celebrating our friend's return," Lila said lazily. Her voice was pure mocking sarcasm when she added, "Fancy seeing you here."

"Oh, we've been discussing trying new places. In fact, it's something of a roommate challenge," Heather Johnson replied. Her makeup was a bit smudged and her dress was a bit crooked. "We've been dared to try the hottest item on the menu."

Vi lifted a brow and glanced at her husband before she asked, "What brought you to this place?"

The friends shrugged, glancing at each other. It was Roman who said, "We often go where the winds take us and then stop. Heather noticed you all coming here on our way to the club and declared she must eat and we must meet the bet."

"How do you keep track of your bets?" Denny demanded. "Do you keep a betting book? Please say that you do. Vi, Lila, I demand we have a betting book. We can keep it next to the gin in the parlor."

Violet bit down on her bottom lip.

"I dare you," Lila told her husband, "to do something worthwhile in the next week."

"Worthwhile?" Denny gasped. "I count helping Vi the other day."

As a group, Vi's friends' gazes shot to Denny except for Vi, who watched for some sort of change in the other group, but they were entirely unperturbed. Vi glanced at Lila and lifted a brow.

Lila smirked as she said, "Heather, my dear, I think you know my mother. Mrs. Lancaster from our home town."

"Do I?"

"Mmm," Rita agreed, leaning in conspiratorially. "I was just visiting with her on my way back from Scotland. When Lila called me home and asked me to check in on her mother, I heard the most delicious tales about you and your friends. You are a bunch of scalawags, aren't you?"

Heather scoffed. "My mother is an inveterate gossip. Did she tell you I barely graduated and it took a little donating? Because that is her favorite story."

Rita laughed. "I didn't even try to go to school beyond finishing school. Violet, you know, and even Lila have both gone to college."

"Only Vi finished," Lila mused.

"And yet, Kate is far more educated than I," Vi shot back.

"Surely not," Jude Brown inserted. "Novelist, financier, crime solver. I have read your books a half dozen times, I think."

"Our books," Victor said. "You'll find all the clever twists are mine."

Vi laughed and then added more food to her plate. They had put all the orders in the center, and she had noted Denny taking much of the paneer tikka masala with a wicked glance at Violet and Rita. "Jack, order some more paneer. Victor, you know that the heart in the books comes from me."

"We've all read them, you know." Barnaby Gallagher sniffed. "I thought that young woman Isla was ridiculous even for a female character."

"She was intended to be," Violet told him. She grinned evilly.

"Based her off of your little sister, didn't you? You can't really miss the similarities after those articles when her betrothed died on her wedding day."

Jack shifted, his arm turning to a protective dead weight.

"My, my, what a fan," Lila mused. She glanced at Rita and then asked, "What else did my mother tell you?"

"Something about a girl that disappeared after you all turned your attention on her. Whatever happened?" Rita turned her big blue eyes on them and then casually added, "In my experience, women of today have more mettle than you'd think, but this one disappeared. Whatever did you do to her?"

The other group of friends glanced between each other and then Heather slowly asked, "Are you referring to Simone Reeves?"

"I am," Rita said, daring a guess. "Some local girl near where you went to school."

"But Barnaby, didn't you say that she went to live with her aunt?" Heather asked, turning. "What's so nefarious about that? So you boys liked her. She was lovely and witty."

"What was she like?" Vi asked, suddenly.

"She was clever," Preston said. "She wasn't educated really, but she forever had a book in her hand, and she knew the oddest little tidbits."

"Tidbits? That's you, Kate."

"She was creative too," Jude said, fervently. "She used to tell ghost stories in the pub, and you'd have shivers for days. Such a fun girl. It's too bad she went off to take care of that aunt of hers. Got conscripted, I think. The female old enough to help and young enough to still order about. Why do you care about some long-gone girl?"

"Where was this?" Rita asked. "Where did you go to school? Were you at Eton and Oxford?"

"Bit rich for our families, I'm afraid."

"Where did you go then?" Violet asked idly, sipping her drink as though her fingers weren't digging into Jack's thigh. She had noticed that he and Ham were leaving the questions to them. Because when Lila and Rita were speaking, and of course Denny, it sounded like mere gossip.

"Durham University," Barnaby said. "Right bore the whole time. I ran through all of my allowance paying for schoolwork."

"Durham?" Ham's head tilted. "Went to school there myself. Did you go to the Dog & Fox? Excellent fish pie."

"Oh fish pie, gah," Preston muttered. "I like a nice pint of stout, a little hearty stew, and some hot rolls."

"We preferred Drunken Monkey." Barnaby laughed. "Haven't thought about that place in so long. They had the meanest old proprietor. Oh, I used to plague him whenever I could."

"Have you tried one of those peppers?" Violet asked Preston. "They're most interesting."

"Interesting?" Preston asked. He reached out and took the red pepper. "It's so shiny. It looks quite refreshing."

"Oh I think you'll remember it," Violet told him idly, and took one herself, popping it into her mouth. She pulled out the stem, smiled with closed mouth, her finger digging even harder into Jack's thigh.

"Oh Vi," Rita said almost as idly. "Try some of my mango lassi."

Violet took Rita's drink just as several of the opposite table reached out for the small red peppers. Vi almost guzzled the milk and mango drink as the gasps from the opposite table started.

"Violet," Lila said low, "I do love you."

"She's my favorite devil," Denny added. "Now for dancing. I declare I need to follow that delightful plate with a few cocktails. Oh!"

Jude Brown was breathing hard, eyes watering, as he guzzled his drink.

"Milk helps," Violet told them softly, waving her hand for the waitress. "They need something cold and milky."

The waitress shook her head. "Your table strikes again. Why anyone trusts you, I don't know."

"At least Vi and Jack tip well." Denny winked at Vi and then said, "Add their bill to ours given they'll be feeling the effects of those peppers for far too long. I shudder to remember my own experience."

Jack snorted, not bothering to hide his wicked amusement. "Let's dance, shall we?"

They rose and none of them were surprised as Jack paid the bills that the other table followed them out.

"Where to next, gents?" Preston asked. "Shall we make a party of it?"

Victor paused too long, but they wanted to see what would happen. Rather than popping Preston a hard hello on the mouth, Victor muttered a reply and ushered his wife ahead of the other group.

CHAPTER 14

"That was just odd," Jack muttered as Hargreaves drove towards the club. "That Jude fellow showed a ridiculous amount of knowledge about your books, but it was all something that anyone who was a fervent fan could know."

"And," Victor added, "the other gents knew about the books. Barnaby for instance."

"And," Vi added, "they didn't seem to be bothered by us asking about Simone Reeves at all."

"Which," Kate put in, "makes you wonder which of them is an incredible actor."

"Or," Vi muttered darkly, "it makes you second-guess yourself."

"Don't be idiotic, Vi," Victor told her. "Whoever drew all those pictures of you, *and only you,* is unhealthily interested in you."

Violet shivered. "If we hadn't searched their house, that interaction wouldn't have been so odd."

"Except they showed up where we did. It wasn't like we made reservations or told someone we were going there. Whoever is doing this either has the cooperation of the group or he's a master manipulator."

Violet glanced out the window. For March, it was drizzly and cold.

"What is most interesting is that because you took those drawings and broke that spyglass, they knew some of us had been in the house. They knew we'd tracked them down as far as we had, and yet they appeared anyway. This isn't a gent who retreats."

Violet tangled her fingers with Jack's and laid her head on his shoulder. They needed to figure out which one of them it could be, or at least rule out someone. Could they rule out Roman Johnson because he had married or did that mean nothing? As much as Violet wished that it could rule him out, she couldn't quite go that far in her mind. Many a man didn't care about his marriage vows. Why would one who didn't care about Vi's privacy or the effects of someone practically hunting her?

She ticked out ideas on her fingers. First, they could use her as bait. She glanced at Jack and knew he'd never willingly do that. But maybe, they could throw one of their spur-of-the-moment parties with dancing and a band and roller-skates in their ballroom? They tended to throw one of those every few months when Victor's excessive wine and spirits purchases strained the limits of their cellars.

Second, they could load up the auto and head into Durham. Could they go there and back in a day? Could they successfully sneak out? Vi glanced at Jack again and made a bet that Ham's questions about which pub they visited were directed with a purpose.

They needed to step forward carefully. The man was someone who hunted them—her—with a totally unobserved aspect. She wasn't exactly unaware of her surroundings after all of the wickedness she'd seen. And yet, she'd been caught blindsided by those early flowers, by the drawing. Every time, it seemed the equivalent of a stranger breaking in on her in the bath. Naked and unarmed. Vi fiddled with her wedding ring.

Third, they could proceed carefully as they were doing and slowly peel away the layers of the residents of the house opposite. How had they gotten the elderly aunt to sign the lease? Was it a fraud? Given that it was Heather's aunt, did that mean that Roman was the fiend after all? Surely, he could be, given it was his mother-in-law who had told Kate's mother about Simone Bates.

Violet sighed, snuggling into his arm. "I feel as though this is the universe counterbalancing my great luck. A good man who loves me, my beloved twin, good friends, even the fortune. We don't have to worry about anything financially and yet all of our money can't tell us who the man is."

"Yet," Jack told her. "Investigations take time. He's got one up on us because he can strike randomly. Sooner or later, we'll catch him."

"And until then, we'll dance and look after each other."

THE CLUB WAS DARK, the strands of lights around the dance floor adding the barest amount of lights. There was the gleaming light of cigarettes for those who danced and smoked and more glints from the candles of the few tables. The stage light was focused on the singer, who looked like a

Scottish shepherdess if you focused only on her face and skin, but her bright lipstick, wailing voice, and shimmering dress transformed her into something otherworldly.

"She's amazing," Violet said to Jack. "We need to get her information so we can hire her for one of our parties."

"The trumpeter is great as well. I could listen to him all night without the others." Jack didn't seem to need more light to know she was tense with stress and developing a headache. He rubbed his hand down her back. "We can take some time for ourselves."

She nodded into his chest, but she didn't really believe it.

"How about you trust me to look after you, and we dance?"

Vi followed him onto the dance floor, and it took her a few songs to lose track of whether the Johnsons and their roommates had arrived. They danced until Jack's gaze was distracted by something that Violet couldn't quite see.

His jaw was flexing as he directed them off the floor. Jack was so tall that he didn't even need to look for the rest of their friends. Instead as they left the floor, they found two tables that had been pushed together. It had Denny and Rita at it.

"Where's everyone?"

"Kate followed Heather to the ladies with Lila."

"Oh," Vi hissed, taking Rita's cocktail and taking a long sip. "Victor?"

"He is lingering near the ladies in case the girls need help," Denny said. "They decided I was a better guard of the table than life and limb."

"We all have our skills," Violet said consolingly. "Did they all come?"

Denny nodded, frowning. "They've been dancing. No one

lingering in the corner with a sketchpad and a sinister expression."

Vi finished Rita's drink while watching the dance floor, looking for the others. It took her a while until she finally spotted Roman dancing with a black woman wearing a gold dress. The woman was out and out gorgeous, and the way Roman's gaze was fixed on her chest, Vi guessed he agreed. A moment later, Vi found Preston Bates, who was circumventing the dance floor with two drinks in his hands. He took a seat a few minutes later next to a girl with marcelled curls that were even more blonde than Rita's.

"Where is Barnaby?"

"Outside, getting air and smoking a cigarette," Ham said, joining them. "He seems to have found a few friends."

"And the other one, Jude?" Jack asked, his tone turning dark and sarcastic as he added, "Vi's biggest fan."

"Funny how he seems to only like Vi's contribution, as though it were possible to tell the difference."

"It's not," Rita said. "Those two, when they go into their writing heads, they might as well be one person rather than two."

"I know," Denny added, grinning at Rita, "a bit uncanny really. You danced with Jude. What did you think?"

"He was boring," Rita answered. "And not even because he was blathering on about you, Vi."

"That would be boring," Vi joked. "I could use something iced and fruity. I am furiously hot."

Jack kissed her forehead and told Ham, "Don't leave her."

"Get me one," Rita and Denny said in unison.

Jack didn't reply, but they didn't need him to reply to know that he would.

"Did you leave Barnaby outside without anyone?"

"Smith's here," Ham muttered. "He'll instigate trouble soon enough, I imagine. Though what he expects to result from it, I don't know."

"Perhaps he thinks that if he ups the pressure someone will either remove themselves from the suspect list or at least push themselves higher."

Vi shook her head, her gaze fixed on the dance floor, so when a hand landed on her shoulder, she screamed.

"Hands off!" Ham ordered as Vi jumped and then moved a chair over to get out of reach of whoever had touched her. She didn't need to look to know it wasn't Jack or Victor.

"Sorry, sorry," Preston said. "I did say your name, but it seemed you were somewhere else. I didn't realize you'd be so jumpy."

"What did you want?" Rita demanded. "By Jove man, you could have just taken a seat rather than scaring her."

"I had no idea that a slight touch would be so alarming. I do apologize, Vi."

"Of course," Vi said, her hand in Denny's. Vi was shaking, to her surprise, and she was using her long-time friend as something of an anchor. "Didn't sleep so well last night," Vi lied. "I fear my dreams were bothering me."

"I apologize again. May I get you a drink?"

Vi shook her head. "Jack is getting me one."

"Yes, well." Preston cleared his throat awkwardly and then took a seat when Ham jerked his head towards one of the empty ones. The silence around the table was almost stifling despite the music from the stage until Rita asked, "And what do you do, Mr. Bates?"

"Uselessly unemployed, I fear."

"I prefer to be useless myself," Denny told him easily. "I

find that it gives me so much time to be useless in different ways. How do you fill your time?"

Preston shrugged. "A little of this. A little of that."

"Ah, I know those pastimes well," Denny said cheerily as though he didn't find the answer irritating. "Do you like the races?"

"I don't gamble," Preston said flatly.

"Cricket?"

"Quite awful at it really. I prefer the sports that don't require a team. I find most of the human race to be lackluster, to be honest."

"What about your roommates?" Rita asked. "I don't have much of a family by birth, but I've joined one here among my friends."

"Oh they're all right, I suppose." He fiddled with the empty glass in front of him as Smith took a seat.

"Hello friends," Smith said wickedly. "However have you been?"

They replied with the usual niceties and then Rita introduced Smith to Preston. As they adjusted, Jude Brown and the Johnsons appeared. Jack was a moment later and then Lila and Kate and finally Barnaby until both groups of friends were crowded around the tables.

"Ah," Smith said. "Jack. Such an interesting evening I've had."

Jack took his seat next to Violet again, taking her hand from Denny and clutching it himself. She started as he did and then glanced at him. She could see the frustration in his gaze. She had been startled enough to latch onto the next ready hand, in this case Denny.

"Oh?" Jack asked, but he didn't seem too interested.

Why were they hiding their thoughts? The man who was

behind all of this knew exactly what they knew. He knew that they were aware that Vi was being observed and possibly hunted. He knew that they'd broken into his house and taken his things. He knew that they were looking. And he had to be amused by their useless flailing.

"Been looking into that little matter you assigned me to."

Jack lifted a brow and shifted, blocking Violet lightly. With the chubby Denny on one side and the mountain of Jack on the other, Violet was almost entirely hidden.

"Oh," Heather asked, sounding excited. "Are you working on another case?"

Victor snorted and Denny giggled as Ham said, "We are, in fact."

"And you all work together?" Roman asked. "Surely that's cheating a bit?"

"Cheating?" Ham asked. "This isn't a game."

CHAPTER 15

*R*oman laughed low and Jack's dark gaze landed on him. Jack, when he was furious, could be terrifying. With a history of military police in the war and hunting killers since he'd been home, Jack's ability to sink into darkness was ever present on the other side of his control.

"You know—" Barnaby said, leaning back with a dark smirk. "I expected more."

"More what?" Denny demanded.

"I've read all those articles about *Lady* Vi, the well-known investigators Hamilton Barnes and Jack Wakefield, and how often you have been notorious. Sounds like a bunch of *spice* journalists write mixed with Lady Vi's fiction."

"You know," Victor sniffed, "I *do* write half of our books."

"Sure you do," Barnaby said, dismissing Victor immediately. "Those books have a lot of female characters."

"You have a bit of problem with females, don't you?"

Smith asked, smiling evilly. "How many have rejected you this evening? It's something of a marvel."

Violet winced as Barnaby's face turned a florid red.

"Do you want to take this outside?" Barnaby asked, knocking his cup over, so it landed on Smith, whose smile turned a slow, almost mischievous evil.

"I would love that," Smith said.

"By Jove, lads," Heather snapped, "control yourselves. School days are over."

"Look at this wannabe trying to slip classes by joining the earl's daughter."

"I am right here," Victor said, lifting his glass to Violet. "We shared a womb, after all, and I am the eldest."

Everyone ignored him except for Vi and Kate, with his wife patting his hand mockingly.

"Slipping classes? It's not me who's slipping classes here." Smith winked at Vi. "Is it, lovely?"

"Here now," Preston said, suddenly sounding furious. "Let's just calm down."

"No," Roman snapped. "Let's watch Barnaby teach this fellow his place with his used suit and his inserting himself where he is not wanted."

"Hey now," Denny said, "Smith is wanted. We *like* him. It's you lot with your clinging ways that make our skins crawl."

"I assure you," Smith said idly, "I could make your skin crawl."

Denny grinned and then huffed out a giggle as he said, "Only in the best way."

"Out!" Barnaby snapped as Vi's party laughed at Denny and Smith. "Out to learn where you belong."

Smith rose along with Barnaby but he was followed by all

of his male friends and Heather groaned. It only took a moment for Denny to leap up, followed by Jack and Ham.

"Jack," Violet muttered. "Don't."

He simply squeezed her shoulder and told Lila, "Stay with her."

"What am I?" Rita demanded. "Chopped liver?"

"You're trouble," Jack told her. "Kate is cultured. Even heavily pregnant, Lila will go in claws out."

"I didn't realize your husband was quite so controlling," Jude murmured low and then followed the group of dueling friends out of the club.

"Let's get our things and go home," Rita murmured. "We'll need to get up early if we're to go to Durham."

Rita had apparently thought through the situation on the drive to the club as well.

Violet nodded, finished her drink, and then followed her friends out to the front of the club. The doorman was watching the ring of men as Barnaby danced about on the toes of his feet, mocking Smith, who was stock still. Barnaby finally feigned forward and Smith simply disappeared. In a swift one-two movement, Barnaby was on the ground and Smith was stepping away as though he'd lifted his hat to a passing lady instead of knocking a man unconscious.

"I find it most effective," Smith said idly, "to stun and then incapacitate. These rich boys with silver spoons in their mouths aren't prepared for real men."

"I say," Roman snarled. "Bad form."

"Bad form?" Violet laughed. "Your friend assumed that because he had been trained somewhat he was capable of fighting whoever he wanted. Surprise," Vi mocked. "Barnaby was wrong."

"So you're turning on us then?" Roman demanded. "Your own kind."

Violet stepped forward into the circle of men and glanced the other group over derisively. "You are not my kind."

Roman lurched forward and knocked into Violet. The next thing Vi knew she was yanked from flailing fists, pushed into Rita's arms, and when she glanced back, there was nothing more than a full fist war with Victor holding onto Jack's back while he kicked one of the other men.

"Jack!" Violet called.

He didn't turn. For the first time, he seemed a stranger to her. She shivered and glanced at Rita, who rolled her eyes and crossed to the man at the door. He went running and came back in mere moments with a bucket of water. Rita stepped into the fray and threw it on the battlers just as the sound of alarms arrived. Before the men had separated themselves from their unexpected bath, local police officers were rounding them up.

Violet shook her head as Jack met her gaze. He was being tugged away by one of the bobbies and Ham was following along without protest. If they weren't going to use their connections, Violet would. She saw both of them look at each other and then shoot silent orders at herself and the other girls. Stay together, be careful. Except their biggest threats were being hauled off as well. That was probably all that was keeping Jack from trying to slide out of trouble and haul Vi towards some bunker.

"Well, lovely," Lila said. "It'll be nice to sleep alone. Denny has cold feet and whines when I use him to heat my own. Plus he's definitely a snuggler and I already have a baby sitting on my bladder."

Vi sighed and then stiffened as Jude and Heather crossed

to join them. Jude Brown had either missed being picked up or he hadn't joined the battle.

"He didn't mean to shove you," Heather snapped. "I suppose they can't have their princess be sullied by us common folk."

Vi lifted a brow and started to reply but Jude beat her to it. "We've all had too much to drink and it was Barnaby who suggested a fight. We both know he assumed he'd be able to smash Vi's friend."

"But—"

"Something is in the air with our friends, Roman included, Heather, and you know it. Let's just take a deep breath and get them all back and tucked into bed. Do you need help, Vi?"

Vi had never given Jude permission to use her first name, let alone her nickname. She supposed that it wasn't so shocking, given their groups had sort of been acquainted since their early days. Instead she shook her head.

"Why are they so protective of you?" Heather hissed. "What is it about you that has your husband asking another woman to look after you? Are you feeble?"

"We look after each other," Rita told Heather flatly. "What is it about you that makes your friends not even look back at you while they were being hauled off by the local bobbies?"

"They know I'm fully capable."

"Or they're just not that attached," Lila said lazily. "Maybe it's like that girl they liked, what was her name?"

"*Simone?*" Heather snorted. "Why do you keep talking about her?"

"You were bothered as well," Kate said softly, "or you wouldn't have told your mother. Especially knowing her mouth is free with the details."

Heather blushed deeply and then let out something of an, "Ack!" before she spun away, snapping at Jude to follow. He hesitated, but his gaze fixed behind Vi and the others. She looked back and found Hargreaves and two of Smith's fellows. They'd shed any resemblance of being servants and looked like the blackguards Vi was sure they were.

"One moment, Hargreaves." Vi turned to the dance club and found the doorman once again. She begged him a favor with a rather large pound note and then was led to the manager's telephone where she called her father and Jack's father and sent them after their friends.

When she stepped out of the office, Jude Brown was waiting. Vi gasped, putting her hand over her heart.

"I didn't mean to startle you," he said softly, reaching towards her just a little. "I just wanted to make sure you really were all right. You were in the midst of things when our friends turned into children."

Violet stepped back. "I'm fine."

Jude's gaze narrowed on her. "Are you afraid of me?"

"Why are you here?" There were so many layers to that question that Violet wanted to throw them at him. Why did your friends follow us to the restaurant and then invite themselves to the same dance club? Why were there so many drawings of me in your house? What happened to Simone Reeves?

"I just wanted to make sure you were all right," he repeated. "You could have been hit and we wouldn't have seen."

"Mr. Brown," Violet said softly. "I am not alone, nor am I helpless."

"I didn't mean to infer you were." His voice was almost a plea. "I apologize. I—I suppose I thought I was being chivalrous. I hope you realize that I don't condone the actions of my friends."

Vi examined his face, wondering if he was the one who had been plaguing her. The plea made her want to weaken, but she could hear Jack's voice in her head telling her to be smarter than that. She glanced up and realized that one of Smith's men was nearby.

"What happened to Simone Reeves?" Vi asked. This time it was her voice that was pleading.

"We told you," Jude said, sounding utterly baffled. "She went off to take care of some aunt. She was just the pub girl, Vi…" He shook his head. "Mrs. Wakefield…I don't understand why you and your friends are fixating on some girl who moved away from her family to take care of an elderly relative. She wasn't important."

"I wonder if you have the right information or I do."

"What is that supposed to mean?" Jude Brown ran his hand through his hair. "I don't understand what is happening here. Or why your friends are being so odd."

"You or one of your friends is watching me, Mr. Brown. He's sending unwanted gifts and drawing pictures that I can assure you I didn't pose for."

Mr. Brown's gaze widened and he stepped back.

"Whoever it was stole my underthings while I was shopping and then you appeared."

"I—" Mr. Brown took another step back. "I—no."

"Why did you show up at the same restaurant where my friends and I were going? Why do you live across the park from me? Who's engineering all of that?"

He started to speak and failed several times before he shook his head helplessly.

"No?" Vi gave him a disgusted look and then sidestepped

him when he went to offer his arm. "I have to go." Before she left, however, she turned back. "Whoever is doing this will be caught."

"Please allow me to make amends for my friends, Mrs. Wakefield." Again that desperation was back in his voice, and she shivered at why he might be so emotionally invested. Was it because he was the villain and thought he was safe? But no, whoever was watching her knew that his drawings had been taken and his spyglass had been broken. Perhaps he was just a good actor.

Vi slid out the club door without answering. She glanced back and noticed that Smith's man was blocking Jude, who despite being uselessly wordless, had followed. Fortunately, Hargreaves was there to escort her to the auto where Smith's other man and the rest of Vi's friends were waiting.

Vi told her friends of Jude's following her to the telephone as they drove back to Vi's house.

"Suspect," Lila declared. "I thought it was him when he showed in the bookstore after your things were taken. This just confirms it for me."

"Yet," Vi said, "he wasn't the one picking fights, and he seemed more afraid than anything."

"True," Kate murmured. "We don't have enough information yet. After this evening, if we discovered it was any one of them, I wouldn't be all that surprised."

"Let's go to Durham tomorrow," Rita said as they reached Vi's house. No one was surprised to see, despite the hour, that the house was attended. As Hargreaves stopped the auto in front of the house, one of the servants came down the stairs to take over the vehicle while Hargreaves accompanied them inside.

The four ladies stared at each other in the hall and then Violet said, "I could use a long, hot bath."

"I'm going to bed," Lila declared.

"Do you need help with the twins?" Vi thought to ask Kate too late.

Kate shook her head and they separated. Violet took a long bath, and when she had changed into pajamas and her favorite kimono, she left her bedroom. It was too late to feel right about waking a servant for a cup of warm milk, but she could make one for herself.

As she walked down the steps, the telephone rang. Vi rushed ahead to the library where it was housed and answered.

"Vi?" The loud voice of her father echoed after her greeting.

"Yes?"

"They aren't being charged but the fellow who is making the decisions refuses to let them go before they spent most of a day realizing how foolish they've been."

"What?" Vi demanded. "But, you're—"

"Turns out the man was more offended by having to face two of the Yard's finest for brawling in the street than myself and he has the power to keep them overnight. They'll be home tomorrow afternoon with ringing ears."

"Lovely," Vi muttered. "Thank you, Father."

Vi hung up the telephone and turned to find Rita. Violet explained, to Rita's disgust.

"You'd think being Yard men would do them some good." Rita adjusted her robe as Vi led the way to the kitchens and started to heat some milk.

"You would think," Vi agreed, adding chocolate to the milk.

"We'll have to go to Durham without them," Rita said.

"We need to leave behind Lila and Kate as well." Vi stirred the milk. "The babies need Kate and Lila would be uncomfortable the entire trip."

"Also, Kate isn't vicious and Lila would be slow if we need to run."

CHAPTER 16

*V*iolet, Rita, and Hargreaves left at dawn despite having gone to bed mere hours before.

"Do you think we're being safe enough?" Violet asked. "If Jack comes home and realizes we're investigating without him, and we weren't safe enough, I will never, *ever* hear the end of it."

"I fear the same could be said of myself and Ham," Rita muttered. She had demanded to be behind the wheel, so poor Hargreaves was in the back with a picnic basket. They should arrive around the time the pub might open as long as they avoided mishaps on the road.

She started out of London by driving deeper into it and taking random turns while Hargreaves watched behind them.

"This is what comes," Violet said darkly as they roved the city, "from marrying men who are not milksops. I could have had a milksop. I could have wrapped Tomas around my finger for the rest of my days and done whatever I wanted with only a, 'yes, dear.'"

"Think, though," Rita said, glancing over at Vi in the front passenger seat, "about how awkward it would have been when he fell in love with your little sister."

A laugh burst from Vi and she saluted Rita. "Too true, my darling friend."

After a good hour of wandering London and a good dozen assurances that they were not being followed, Rita headed the auto towards Durham. As early as they'd left, it was past noon before they arrived in Durham, given their need to shake a possible tail.

"Do you think that because there's no one following us, it means that our culprit is in jail with Ham and the others?" Rita asked as they passed through yet another little village. She gestured outside of the window and announced, "This place is quaint in all the best ways."

Vi only answered the first part of Rita's comment. "No. I revealed our hand to Mr. Brown. He may well be trying something different. Or he knows that if he follows us while everyone else is incarcerated that we'll have our man."

They rode in silence for a while with Vi reading over the notes she'd made on the chalkboard and transcribed to her journal. She had no further conclusions after re-reading the journal and wondered if she should consider making a time-line for each person. Only, she had no idea what drew the man to her.

Was it articles written about her? Was it someone she'd known for years like Preston Brown. Known and ignored? Ignored was too much credit really, Vi thought. She'd been oblivious to him and possibly the rest of them since her schoolgirl days. She had nothing to prove that the person who'd turned his attention to her had done so a long time ago, after reading her books, or because he'd passed her in the park. Since she had no idea, a timeline was useless.

When they arrived in Durham, the drizzle had turned to a downpour, and it took far longer than expected to find the pub. It was tucked into an out-of-the-way side street and the noon rush was on. The pub tables were thick with students, along with a few grizzled old men who resolutely ignored the much younger patrons.

Rather than trying to find someone who would talk to them during the lunch rush of fish and chips, they joined the queue, ordering lunch and pints and finding a table in the corner.

Violet bit into the fish with little appetite. Her husband and her twin were in jail. Potentially with the same fellow who was hunting her. It was time to do something, but she still wasn't sure what to do. They could...what...stalk the members of the other house in reverse? But Vi paused. She was suddenly certain that Smith had been doing just that.

They finished their fish, chips, and mushy peas while the pub was still busy and then lingered over a second pint as they watched the pub slowly empty. Vi and Rita rose, leaving Hargreaves at the table, and approached the bar. The man working had handlebar mustaches, thick wrinkles at the corners of his mouth, and beefy arms that shocked Violet. Jack was the largest man that Vi knew, and he was certainly taller than this man, but the fellow's arms were tree trunks.

"Hullo, hullo," Violet said, grinning merrily despite the anxiousness welling in her. She knew that Simone Reeves had worked at the pub and hoped that they knew her family. "I'm looking for Mr. Reeves?"

The man eyed her as though she were a foreign bit of

something in his plate. He glanced beyond her to Rita and then back again. "You seem a bit fine for this place. Bit fine for ole Paddy Reeves too."

Vi glanced down at her dress. It was light blue, bordered in a dark blue and cut at an angle. Rita was even finer in her cream, beaded day dress and the jaunty hat with the long cream feather.

"And yet," Rita said, using a similarly merry tone as Vi's, "we're supplicants."

"I'm Paddy Reeves."

Violet started to speak and then to her surprise her eyes welled with tears. She needed to verbalize what had been happening to her and to ask for help and instead she was choking. She dug her handkerchief out of her pocket while Rita took over.

"This is my friend, Violet Wakefield. We think you may have some insight into a trial she's experiencing."

"Fancy type like you?" Paddy shrugged and wiped his cloth over the bar. "Doubt it."

"We heard your sister? Daughter? I don't know. Simone?"

Paddy's face went from idly curious to a stone wall.

Rita, however, pressed on. "We were trying to find some information about some people who'd come into our lives and her name came up."

Paddy crossed his arms over his chest. He said nothing, but his gaze was hot and furious.

"Violet, like we believe happened to Simone, is being harassed by one of those people. We've narrowed down where they live and have a short list of names, but—well, we don't even know if this fellow is a distant admirer or a foe."

"Foe," Paddy grunted. His throat croaked, and his gaze

met Vi's. Both of them were tearful. "If he's the same one, he's a foe, miss."

With shaking hands, Violet slowly opened her journal and put a drawing in front of Paddy. His gaze widened and he nodded, head moving fast, as he swallowed repeatedly.

"The same. The same for my girl."

Vi bit down on her bottom lip, glancing back at Hargreaves. "I'm so sorry to ask, but what happened to her? Simone?"

"The worst, save death," Paddy said, clearing his throat darkly.

Rita gasped, but as much as Vi had held out hope, she was unsurprised.

"Did she identify who hurt her?"

"He took her with chloroform, we think. He hadn't bound her, so the first chance she got, she ran. Came home to us, locked herself in her room, and refused to leave."

"Did you have any clues?"

Paddy Reeves slowly shook his head. "Wish I could say that I had some, Miss Wakefield, but I don't. It started with love letters left on the bar. Then little tokens. Flowers and things. At first, Simone was flattered. Excited even."

Vi nodded. "Flowers for me, first. But it came with a too expensive piece of jewelry."

"Not for Simone. But she wasn't fancy like you. Just a girl who worked in her father's pub."

"What happened next? After the trinkets?"

"Letters that referenced things a casual admirer wouldn't know. It was clear he'd been watching her. I didn't like it from the beginning, but Simone was spooked at that point."

Violet took a long breath in and asked, "What happened

to her then? We questioned the suspects and they all claimed she went to her aunt. They were acting like we were crazy."

Paddy Reeves eyed Violet for a long time and then just shook his head.

Vi paused and then asked, "May I dare to hope she's all right?"

Again, Paddy Reeves didn't answer. Vi could only hope that the reason for that was because he had someone to protect. Simone, in fact. Violet pulled her diamond earbobs from her ears and told him, "These are for her. If you take them to Rose and Blacke in London and tell them I sent you, they'll give you a good price."

"I didn't say she was around. I'm not for sale."

Violet reached out and took his hand. "I have more than I need, and if I had to start over with nothing, a helping hand from another victim would be welcome."

Reeves's face did not adjust at all.

"Can you help us rule out any of these names?"

Violet handed over her journal and Reeves read their notes.

He cleared his throat and then said, "I thought it was this Roman Johnson fellow despite that blonde who hung on his arm as though he were the good Lord."

Paddy glanced behind him and then said low, "I was tired of my girl being terrified. I was tired of waking to her screams. I was just tired."

"Whatever you did is safe with us," Rita told him. "If it helps, we *will* find him."

"How can you be so sure?"

"Violet Wakefield is married to one of the best Scotland Yard men who is like brothers with another of the best Scotland Yard men. They have mountains of money, and the wit to use it well."

Paddy Reeves eyed Violet and then, voice hoarse again, he said, "You'll tell me when you've found him?"

Vi nodded instantly.

"It would be a relief. For *all* involved."

"I will do whatever I can for her," Vi's head tilted and she admitted, "*and* myself."

"I thought it was Roman Johnson because I thought I saw him deliver one of the little notes. I beat him within an inch of his life and left him in a gutter. Simone was taken while he was still in hospital."

"What about this Barnaby Gallagher?"

"Is he the one with the massive mole on his chin?" Reeves fingered his jaw line. "The bookworm? Or the tubby one?"

"The tubby one," Violet admitted.

"Simone felt the man's chest and arms. She was sure he didn't have a bit of fat on him."

Vi nodded, because it was too hard to speak. She could only imagine how horrifying it had been for Simone to think back on what happened to her, to think about the body that had forced itself on her and only been able to rule out the chubbier of the possibilities.

"Both Preston and Jude are quite thin," Rita muttered. "I say we take them, tie them to a chair, and beat it out of them."

"I concur," Reeves muttered. "I'll be your fists if you'll be my alibi."

"Agreed," Rita said, giving him an evil grin.

"Bloody hell," Vi breathed. "Do you know how many times I've walked in my garden at night? Or in the park alone?"

"There's a reason Jack bought those terrifying guard dogs when you were being pranked. I suppose I should prepare myself for some as well. I wouldn't be surprised if Ham didn't suggest them to Jack."

Violet reached across the bar and hugged Paddy Reeves tight.

"I'll be back," she whispered. "In a moment and then later with the name and freedom for Simone. Is your wife still around?"

He nodded. "Neither of us have ever been the same."

Vi gathered Hargreaves with a glance and then wandered through Durham until she found a little shop. Vi randomly added items to a basket, shopping almost blindly. She couldn't do anything for Simone, her mother, or her father. Not yet, not until she found the fiend, but she could at least show that someone cared with a few luxuries.

Rita watched Vi carefully and then helped. Soon, in a rush through stores, Hargreaves had been loaded down with soft wool wraps, pretty scarves, boxes of chocolate, fine brandy, embroidered silk, specialty tea blends, and Violet's favorite—ginger wine.

When they returned to the pub, Vi saw that Mr. Reeves had been joined by a woman behind the bar. She had brilliant huge brown eyes, deep brown hair, fine pale skin, and sharp features.

"She looks a bit like how I would imagine your mother to look, Vi."

Violet had paused when she took in the face and had to force herself to move closer. Rita was right. This woman could have been Vi if twenty years were added to her age and a weight of sadness had been in her eyes.

"Oh Paddy," the woman said. Her accent was lightly

French and she rounded the counter to take Vi's face between her hands. "You look so like her. If I'd had a second daughter, she might have looked like you."

Vi had to bite down on her bottom lip to keep herself from leaning into Mrs. Reeves's arms and begging to be held. Only Vi didn't have to ask. Mrs. Reeves wrapped warm, loving, *mother's* arms around Violet, slowing caressing Vi's hair as Mrs. Reeves hummed low.

"There, there darling. It'll be all right."

Vi closed her eyes and breathed in the love. She had so missed a mother's love after losing her mother and then her Aunt Agatha. She was shaking when she finally pulled back.

"Thank you," Vi told her.

"Paddy believes you can make our Simone safe again." The voice was a low whisper and Mrs. Reeves carefully ensured that no one could hear her speak.

"I can." Vi's statement was nothing more than a binding oath. "I will."

"I believe you will," Mrs. Reeves said, taking Vi's face between her hands again. The almost matching dark gazes locked and then Mrs. Reeves kissed Vi on each cheek and stepped back. Neither of them acknowledged the load of gifts and Violet left with a second promise that they would hear from her soon.

CHAPTER 17

"I would wring your neck if I thought you'd been foolish," Jack swore against Vi's hair after they reached the London house. He breathed her in, holding her tight, and muttered, "It was me who was. Smith was free and clear. And I was locked away while a possible villain was also free."

"I'm fine," Violet told him, avoiding the confirmation that she'd seen Jude Brown when Jack had been taken away. After long moments, Vi pulled back. They eyed each other and then Vi said, "We've narrowed it down to Preston or Jude."

"Did you find out what happened to Simone Reeves?" Smith demanded. He was leaning back in one of the chairs near the fire, utterly comfortable in the tuxedo from the night before. In his hand was a martini with several olives and near the bar was her twin making another round of drinks.

Vi nodded, but she couldn't say it. She didn't want to hear

it again or acknowledge that it was true, so she glanced at Hargreaves and said, "I need to freshen up."

Vi fled up the stairs and filled the bath, scrubbing her skin raw even though the victim of the crime had been Simone. When Vi dressed again, she wore long navy sleeves that reached just past her wrists. The dress was cut in a long swathe of navy fabric that shimmered with silver thread and had been her choice for the last dinner with her father and stepmother. Her back was bare, but Vi added a navy silk wrap that hid her skin.

Given the dress covered her nearly to her ankles, and that she'd left off the makeup and jewelry and slapped a turban over her wet hair, she had little doubt she'd be advertising her discomfort to everyone in her house.

She returned to the parlor as the dinner gong rang and found that everyone had changed except for Smith, who shot her a challenging look. Vi ignored him and let Jack lead her to the dining room.

"So, we're working with the two cousins." Smith tilted his head. "Do you know, Johnson and I bonded in jail."

"Did you?"

"Told him I'd been doing a spot of investigating for you. Told him I knew about the lease on the house. Told him I expected he'd soon discover the house had been purchased by Wakefield and they'd be evicted."

"Did you?" Vi demanded, turning her attention to Jack.

He shrugged, but the look on his face told her he was more worried she hadn't thought of it herself. Vi shivered. He wasn't wrong.

"I thought we could give it to Isolde and Tomas."

"Give?" Denny demanded. "Give it to Lila and I. Tomas is

ever fleeing your stepmother and has his own oversized, ancient mansion."

"You can have it cheap," Violet told him. "Now shut up. What did Johnson say to that?"

"Funny thing," Smith answered. "He didn't know anything about it. He said the house had been taken by that Brown fellow. Got to questioning him a bit further and Johnson said that Brown had always been a bit squirrelly. Said Brown had been the one to bring home the *bedamned* dogs. Said Brown was always wandering about, nose in a book. Johnson said, in fact, that Brown was the type of fellow to realize what was happening around him far more so than one would expect."

"It's Brown?" Lila almost crowed. "I said it was. I feel like I should certainly get a prize."

Gazes turned Lila's way were not nearly as amused and she scrunched up her nose.

"No time to be jolly, darling," Denny told her in a sarcastic stage whisper. "We've a devil on our hands and have yet to catch him in something to put him away."

"Also," Smith said, "I tend to disbelieve everything I hear from these suspect types. Or fools like you, Denny."

Vi rubbed her brow. Her head had been aching since they returned to the auto and motored back to London. The pain had seemed to intensify with each mile that passed, every instinct screaming at her to run away.

"We've options here," Smith said.

"We can leave," Ham immediately answered. "Perhaps go and join Rita's father at the property he bought in Scotland. It's a ridiculous old place, but they do have good fishing."

"We could lay a trap," Victor said. "Do you think I could pass for Vi? Because, pretty devil, you won't be the bait."

Rita shoved her untouched plate away and lifted her wine glass, taking a sip before she said, "You know what bothers me?" She glanced around the table and then answered, "The way Paddy Reeves referred to his daughter as though she were dead."

Vi blinked and thought back. Mr. Reeves had referred to her in past tense. Yet Vi was almost certain Simone was alive.

"People lie," Smith said. "Perhaps we should look into this Reeves character."

"I don't think the hope on their faces when we said we'd catch him and see him punished was a lie. I think that they told people Simone had gone away, but they talked about her in past tense to keep our man from looking. The truth is she's alive. The truth is also they believed that he would have followed her if he knew where she was. At least before Vi."

Vi rapidly reassessed her thoughts and then reached the conclusion Rita wanted them to reach. "If I run, I might find myself chloroformed somewhere where I thought I was safe."

"Yes," Rita agreed. "I don't think anyone knows where we went. So, they can't know that we know what happened to Simone. That's to our advantage. We *could* lay a trap. Because they know we're on guard, but they don't know exactly how seriously we're taking this."

Jack had said nothing, and Violet almost thought he wasn't listening except for the fury in his gaze. He'd been nearly silent since she'd returned, covered like a nun, from her bedroom. She hadn't met his gaze, and he hadn't tried to catch hers. There was this divide between them, but it wasn't that they weren't united. He imagined Vi as the victim instead of Simone. And Vi knew the story would agonize and haunt him. She wasn't capable of squelching her own fears in the face of his. She'd weep, he'd turn nearly as mad as he had been the night before, and they'd have a disaster on their hands.

Vi reached out and took his hand, curling up in her chair with her ginger wine, and looked around the table.

"Now that we have faces," Violet told them. "We could revisit the flower shops and see which man is recognized."

"Yes," Denny announced. "Excellent plan. Please don't erupt, Jack."

Jack only acknowledged Denny with the flicker of an eyelid.

"With the guard dogs," Victor started softly, "all of us in the same house, Smith's men, your own loyal servants, I think we're as safe as possible while in the house."

"She can't stay in the house forever," Kate told him. "Nor can she consider herself safe. How do we get this man to do something that will put him away? We *need* him to attack."

"Or," Smith added, "we could remove them both from the situation."

"We're not murdering anyone." Ham glanced at Jack almost apologetically and then amended, "At least without trying everything else first."

"Attack is a good plan. You won't pass for Vi," Jack told Victor. "But there's a secretary who works for the Yard who could with the right dress, the right hat, and a veil."

"Brigid?" Ham asked low. "That's asking a lot."

"We can reward her far beyond anything the Yard would."

"She's having trouble paying for her rooms," Ham told Jack.

"Vi owns swanky rooms in that estate of hers. Give one to the girl for free."

"If that's what she wanted," Vi agreed.

Silence fell on the table as they considered just *how* they'd get the man to strike.

"He's shown himself to be something of an excellent hunter." Jack was speaking to Ham more than anyone else. "I think he might sense a trap."

"I could just break into their rooms and search them more thoroughly," Smith offered.

Jack shook his head. "This man is too clever for that. Everything we found that was evidence in your search, in Vi's, was in a room that any of them could be using."

"I think we should kidnap them, torture them, and then strip the victim of funds and identification and ship him to Mongolia under the care of someone who will dump him in a gutter bloody and alone." Smith lifted a brow and then added, "We need to get this resolved before Beatrice returns. She'll dive right into Vi's troubles, and she's here alone when the rest of you are gone."

Violet fiddled with her wedding ring and then returned to her journal, which she'd set on the floor next to her chair. She opened the pages and re-read what they knew about Preston Bates and Jude Brown, reading the old one and then creating a new entry based off of the more recent information.

PRESTON BATES — Lives off of a small inheritance and gambling winnings. Associated with a group of friends who already drove Simone Reeves and her family into hiding her. He won money from the rogue Theodophilus Smythe-Hill. Had Theo met his match in Preston?

Preston and Jude were raised in the same house. Was Jude's fearful alarm when Vi confronted him because he knew exactly what Preston was? Maybe he'd even seen it before Simone. Jude claimed that Preston was around when Vi's underthings were stolen. Had he engineered why they were by the boutique where Vi, Lila, and Kate were shopping. If he really was around, where had he been in between disappearing from the boutique and when Vi entered the bookshop?

Received the flower that first drew Vi's attention to him and his party. Was he an unwitting victim or had that been his purpose all along?

JUDE BROWN — Raised with Preston Bates. Appeared at the bookstore directly after when Violet's underthings were stolen nearby. He seems to know rather a lot about Vi through her books. He doesn't work and is something of an intellectual. A first in mathematics is nothing to discount. Why doesn't he have to work? Does he have some other inheritance?

When he ran into Vi at the bookstore, why did he arrive after Vi? Was he the one who stole Vi's underthings and then was clever enough to pretend Preston was around?

QUESTIONS —

Simone had been flattered when she first started receiving notes and tokens. Why didn't the fellow just introduce himself and romance her? What was the purpose in slowly scaring her and then taking her?

They'd searched the house and hadn't found Vi's underthings. If they searched again, would they find them?

Could anything they found after they revealed themselves be sufficient to prove anything? This fellow was clever. Surely anything they found could be a plant to frame someone else.

Vi SHOWED Jack her notes and he read them over and sounded worn down when he told her, "The reason this fellow didn't romance her and instead took her and abused her is because he's not interested in love. He wanted Simone afraid, Vi. She was probably as vibrant as you, and the game was to dim that light and turn her into a shadow of herself."

Vi stared at him and then glanced down at the armor she'd put on that covered every inch of her skin. She'd left off her makeup, her jewelry, the things she generally enjoyed and covered herself as though it were her fault that she'd garnered this man's attention. Her frown deepened, but her fingers remained tangled in Jack's.

"After this," Vi told him, "we're going to try a series of new adventures."

His eyes glinted at her declaration and her fierce tone. "Whatever you want to do," he promised.

"This will be over soon," she promised in return. "Things will go back to normal, and we'll shake it off as though it never happened. This man is using anonymity and shock to scare us. But we're better than this."

"Hear, hear," Ham replied. "Rita and I will join you on some of those adventures."

"In between, of course," Denny added, giggling, "working for Smith."

CHAPTER 18

$\mathcal{A}$nother bouquet of flowers arrived three days later with another sketch. This one said:

Constantly in my thoughts.
  —Yours

The drawing underneath left nothing to the imagination. The best that could be said of it was that her leg was lifted in a way that only her chest was on full display. She would have gasped if she hadn't seen the other drawings, but she was growing numb to the shock and she only felt disgust.

The bouquet was full of peach blossoms. Vi stared at them, letting her finger trace over the delicate pink flowers instead of drawing back from them. She wasn't going to let flowers unsettle her. She glanced at Jack, waiting. Peach blossoms were not a flower she knew the meaning of and given the look on Jack's face, she wasn't going to like it.

"What does it mean?" Vi asked softly.

His jaw flexed and his hands were clenched with the small book starting to crumple under the force of his fingers.

"Jack?" Vi approached him, wrapping her arm around him. He glanced at the door where the delivery boy was standing in hope of a tip, and then Jack gave Violet the most obscure look when he spoke.

"Who have you enslaved, Violet? How long am I going to have to deal with this madness? I didn't marry you to watch you pull everyone into your orbit and expect the whole world to worship at *Lady* Violet's feet."

Vi stepped back, her gaze wide. She wasn't acting. Having Jack turn the force of his fury on her, something he'd never done, had sent her heart to racing and her eyes to welling even though she knew he was acting for the sake of the delivery boy.

"I—" Vi's bottom lip trembled. "I—don't know what you mean. I didn't do anything."

"Of course you didn't," Jack snarled. "All these flowers, the jewels, the drawings. Of *course* you weren't out flaunting yourself. Tell me, Violet, how does he know how to draw you?"

"I don't know," Vi wailed, trying not to flinch. It wasn't her. It had been drawn with the idea that she was more voluptuous than she was. She had a bit of curve—it wasn't like she looked like a boy—but she didn't have the attributes of that drawing.

Jack threw the picture into the fire, and she barely held back the shudder of relief that it was gone from the world.

"I'm tired of this, Violet." This time the heat was gone from his voice. It was cold, chilling even in the acting, and she shivered. "Make it stop."

He stormed from the room, and Violet turned her tear-filled eyes to the delivery boy and then to Hargreaves, who had lost all ability to pretend to have no reaction to what he had seen.

"Tip him," Violet pleaded to Hargreaves and then fled up the stairs. She didn't call Jack's name, and she didn't pretend she wasn't upset. She just rushed away as though she were devastated. She hurried into their bedroom, closed the door, and wandered weakly to sit on the side of the bed.

She breathed in slow, reminded herself Jack was acting, and breathed out even more slowly. It took a few more breaths than she'd expected, since she knew it hadn't been real, and when she looked up he was standing in the doorway to the bathroom. The self-loathing on his face was enough for her to dart across the bedroom and leap into his arms.

"I'm sorry," he swore against her hair. "Never again."

She shook her head, clutching his neck as she countered, "As many times as it takes to sell a division between us so this can be over."

"No. Never. I don't ever want to do that to you again."

Violet curled her fingers into his hair until the door to their bedroom opened. Her twin stepped inside. "Heard a bit of that."

"It was an act," Violet told him flatly.

"I know," Victor said easily. "Just wondered if I needed to tell you that Smith's man followed the flower boy, and he cut back towards the house across the park. It seems that the reason you were never able to identify who was buying the flowers was because they were being purchased by someone who both bought in disguise and hired his own delivery boys."

Jack turned, still holding Violet and then muttered, "It had better have been good for something. She cried."

"She's always been a bit emotional." Victor chucked her on the shoulder and then said, "It was pretty convincing."

"I channeled my rage at our man. I might need you to prevent me from killing him, Victor. I want nothing more than to wrap my fingers around his neck and squeeze, watching him struggle for air as he realizes that he'll never have any again."

"Ah," Victor said, blinking rapidly at the descriptive murder plans. "All right."

"Don't fail," Violet told him.

"I won't," he swore, then his expression hardened. "I don't like how this monster is fixated on you. I don't like how he's hunting you. I don't like those drawings. And I don't like that you're nothing more than a type to him. You look like Simone. For all we know, Simone looked like someone else. Someone has...has...fixated his madness on you, and we're going to teach him the error of his ways."

His tone was so fierce, so protective, so angry, that Violet looked to Jack and told him, "You'll need to prevent my brother from committing murder as well." She closed her eyes with a sigh. "This waiting is getting to me."

ON THE NEXT MORNING, with a rare sunny sky overhead, Rita and Ham rose early, took his dogs, and left carrying a blanket and a large picnic basket. Vi waved at them from the doorway and then ran outside to hand them two bottles of champagne. They were going to the location where Brigid would soon follow to help set up the trap for their foe.

It had been orchestrated to ensure that anyone watching thought Vi was still in the house. A few hours later, Lila and Kate left with one of Smith's men. They were followed by the servants leaving in a group for their half-day.

Victor and Denny left next, dressed for cricket and carrying bats. It was then that Violet and Jack took her dogs into the park. They started out arm-in-arm, heads tilted together as though they were happy as ever.

"Back off some now," Jack told her after they'd walked for at least an hour, "as though I've said something mean."

Vi jerked back from him, barely keeping her hand on his arm. She paused to look up at him and hissed, "I am saying so many mean things right now, it's ridiculous."

"You're ridiculous," Jack shot back, scowling at her. "When all of this is over, I think we should escape for a long weekend in Paris where we'll indulge in all of the things available."

"Without Denny," Vi said, shoving his arm from her and putting her other hand on her neck. Her eyes were wide and hurt as she added, "He's been giggling far too much lately. I think the pressure of becoming a father is making him giddy."

"It'll be a romantic getaway. Perhaps we should follow it up with a week in Nice."

Vi gasped. "It'll be far too cold. Let's go somewhere warmer."

"Agreed," Jack growled. "Then we'll go to the country and ride horses, have afternoon naps, and possibly indulge in some of Victor's blackberry cordial."

Vi took a step back, holding her hand over her mouth. "He's the spoilt son of an earl. We need to find his former supplier and get a bottle from her as well to compare the two."

"I don't know," Jack shot back, throwing his arms in the air. "No one knows more about spirits than him."

Vi turned on him, taking both dog leashes and running towards the house. She darted up the steps and slammed the door behind her, locking it.

Then she met the gaze of a woman with dark hair and dark eyes and of a similar height as Vi.

"Hopefully we pulled that off." Violet grinned at Brigid. Vi took off her red coat and grey cloche along with the thick scarf about her neck.

"It looked quite fraught, ma'am." Vi adjusted her decoy's hat as the woman buttoned up the coat and knotted the scarf high around her throat.

Hargreaves came to stand behind Brigid as Jack started banging on the door.

"Violet," he shouted. "Violet Wakefield, open this door or I'm going to wring your neck!"

Vi glanced at Hargreaves and whispered, "Aren't you supposed to be on your half-day?"

"You weren't the only one bribed to stay out of the next part," Hargreaves told her simply as Jack pounded on the door again and then cursed loudly before stomping down the steps. Vi peeked through the peephole and saw he was gone. A moment later a black cab pulled up outside of the house. "My duty is with you ma'am."

"You're on," Violet told Brigid.

The woman patted Vi's red handbag where she had put a pistol. Jack had tried to loan her one, but she'd pulled one from her own handbag, loaded it with skilled movements, and tucked it into Vi's handbag. Jack had been smiling by the end, but Brigid merely looked professional.

Vi caught her arm before she turned away. "Thank you, Brigid."

Brigid winked and said, "Having a set of my own rooms will change my whole life, my lady. What's a little playacting?"

Vi stepped into the shadows, tugging the dogs—still on their leashes—with her. Brigid placed a handkerchief over her face as though she were sobbing into it and then darted out the door and down the steps into the black cab driven by Smith himself, though hardly recognizable in his uniform. The door slammed behind Brigid and then the auto sped away.

Jack came into the room from another part of the house. He tugged Violet close, kissed her soundly, and said, "Hopefully we'll catch our man."

"And then Paris," Violet swore.

"Paris," he agreed, pressing the gentlest of kisses to her forehead. "Be careful." A moment later, he ran after the black cab, shaking his fist, and then darted down the street to hail another, this one driven by Ham, also in disguise.

"Do you think it will work?" Vi asked Hargreaves.

He nodded, his gaze sympathetic, but then he added, "Nothing is going to happen to you, Mrs. Vi. Not from a man like this. Not on our watch. Come, we need to head out the back. Lila and Kate are waiting for us."

Vi smiled at him, not knowing what else to say. She was feeling irrationally guilty that Simone Reeves hadn't had the same care. Let alone guilty that she had put this much stress on her friends and family even though she knew that they blamed only the perpetrator, and even drawn in an innocent woman to help them, though Brigid seemed more than capable at taking care of herself. Was it likely that Brigid was hoping to be more than a simple secretary at Scotland Yard?

"The pistol was left for you in the library," Hargreaves said.

"The pistol, out the back, to the auto, and to drive aimlessly occasionally bypassing Scotland Yard and looking for Jack, Ham, or Victor. Simple enough I suppose, though I object to being left out."

Violet followed him to the library and then paused. She had been persuaded to stay out of the thick of things, so that whoever was behind this wouldn't have a chance to get their hands on her. Hargreaves had locked the front door, the house was safe, and the guard dogs were strutting about the garden. Nothing more could be done but to fulfill her boring part of the bargain.

When she reached the library, the fire was burning, there was a basket filled with treats, chocolates and books, and she could see the touches of those who loved her. Hargreaves picked up the cozy blanket from Jack who knew she tended to shiver when spooked. The chocolates from Denny and Lila, though Lila would certainly eat half the box while they wandered London. The books from Victor and Kate. There was quite a serviceable lady's revolver next to the basket from Rita and Ham.

Hargreaves took up the basket and the blanket and Vi winked at him, sliding her hand into the crook of his elbow and holding the leashes of both dogs. The revolver had already made its way to her pocket.

She couldn't help but think it must be Jude Brown. He had been in the bookshop just after her underthings had been stolen. He knew too much about her. Things that a normal fan of her writing wouldn't know. Or perhaps only the most obsessive of fans, but what were the chances that the most obsessive of fans wasn't also the person leaving the unwanted letters, making the drawings, and generally terrifying her.

Either way, it would all be over soon, she thought, and then Paris, somewhere warm, and refuge in their country house. The swimming pool they'd added should be finished by the time they returned, and they'd be able to indulge themselves as a family.

CHAPTER 19

*I*t was Holmes who alerted them that something was amiss. His head lifted suddenly and he whined. His gaze was turned towards the front of the house, and Vi shivered. They had just left the library and were moving quickly towards the back of the house when Holmes adjusted from alert to a low whine. They froze.

There it was, a telltale scratch. Perhaps only possible because the library was so close to the front door and because of the dog clueing them in. Vi's head tilted as she heard it again. Whoever it was, wasn't even trying to hide their entrance.

"Oh no," Hargreaves said. "We should run."

"That little alley between my house and Victor's is a long stretch of a trap."

Hargreaves closed his eyes and then said, "My lady, hide yourself."

Violet ignored him, rushing back into the library and

grabbing the telephone. She listened to the line phone and there was nothing. They had been cutoff.

"Whatever you need," Hargreaves swore.

"Run for Lila and Kate and get help."

"No!" he told her. "You go there, and I'll stop the man."

"No," Violet said and then they both froze when they heard the crash of something breaking.

"It's too late," Hargreaves said, locking the library door. They eyed each other. The man had been so fast, he must not have bought a single piece of the day's playacting. Did he know that Lila and Kate were waiting in an auto round the side of Victor's house? Did the man know that the only time she would be only partially unprotected was because everyone else was setting the trap to entice him into a crime that would send him to prison?

"Violet," a low voice called. "Violet, my darling. I'm here."

Vi gulped, steeling her spine.

"Take the servants' stairs," Hargreaves commanded in a rare show of disobedience. "Get out. I'll hold him off."

"No." Vi took the dogs and put them in a closet, blocking them from exiting. She hissed a command of, "Quiet," and only a low whimper could be heard. "We'll do this together."

"Violet," the voice called again, shaking the handles of the library door. "I know that wasn't you. I haven't fallen for your little sideshow act."

Vi clenched her fists. Paris was ahead, happiness, and the freedom to leave her house without worrying. She glanced around and then saw the revolver left by Rita and Ham. Bless them for assuming things could go awry.

Vi grabbed the gun and then a fireplace poker and slid behind the door. Hargreaves took the other side. She breathed in slowly as the man called her name again.

"Here now!" someone called from outside and the scratching at the library door stopped. "What are you doing? Get out of here."

To Vi's horror, the only answer was the sound of a gunshot.

"Smith's man. There should be another with Lila and Kate. They may have heard."

"Look what you've made me do, my angel. Enough of this. We've only so long before they realize I slipped their trap and have come for you."

Vi's hands were shaking as the sound of scratching at the door started again. It took long, long minutes for him to open the door and he was cursing at her by the time he burst through. He seemed to prognosticate that she'd be behind the door and ready with a fireplace poker. As she swung it down on him, he caught it and then used it to tug her close.

Hargreaves held out his gun and demanded, "Let her go!"

Instead of replying, Preston Bates shot Hargreaves. Vi screamed as he fell and then her gaze turned to the fiend. Her face was smashed against the mole on his chin as Bates hissed, "That's not how we behave."

Vi's answer was to press the revolver into his side and pull the trigger.

His dark eyes widened in shock as he grabbed his side where the blood was already spreading. Violet didn't wait. She raced out the door chased by the sound of him stumbling behind her and cursing.

A shot echoed past her just as she dove down the front steps, sending a burning pain through her shoulder, but she didn't hesitate. She ran ahead, adding a zigzag to her route, pulling from one of Victor's contributions to their books.

She zigzagged out the front gate and then threw herself to the side where the brick pillar hid her from another shot.

Panting, she looked up as the local bobby came running across the park, followed by a limping Jude Brown. Their gazes met, and he shouted something her way. She heard nothing but the pounding of her own heart as she slowly turned back to the gateway, transferring the gun from her injured hand to her uninjured one. Vi said a swift, terrible prayer to stay with her family before she pushed to her feet and aimed the revolver at Preston Bates.

"My love?" he asked her, baffled, but also angry. Did he really have no idea how she felt? How any woman would feel?

Vi's answer was another shot. Her shot was followed by sirens and then the bobby was tugging her gun arm away as Preston fell to his knees. Vi would have shot him again, but the revolver Rita left only had two shots. She wanted to dive at him, and she was pretty sure she did given the way the bobby was hauling her back.

"There's an injured servant inside," Violet finally ground out. "He needs help."

If the bobby replied, Violet didn't hear it. She could see Jude speaking to her, but she couldn't quite respond. Her hands were shaking and she was shivering and she was barely aware that her arm was bleeding until Hargreaves knelt in front of her, gently taking her face between his hands. She hadn't been aware she'd slipped to the ground.

"You're all right," he told her, and then wrapped a blanket around her shoulders. "Everything is just fine."

"Are you all right?" she demanded. "I thought you were dead."

"I hit my head on the way down," he told her. "Just a little shoulder wound."

Vi blinked at him and then looked down. Holmes and Rouge had followed Hargreaves out, and they were pressed against her body, shaking nearly as badly as she was. She reached out to pet Rouge and realized that blood had poured down her arm.

"I've been shot," Vi said stupidly.

"Just a flesh wound," he told her gently. "We'll be matching in our slings."

For some reason, she found that hysterically funny and she started giggling. The bobby asked Hargreaves something, and to her shock he snapped at the man.

"You sound angry," she said softly. "It'll be all right."

Hargreaves nodded, his eyes shining as he took off his cravat and used it on her arm. She gasped as he tightened it down.

"You were the hero, my lady. You got the man and saved us both."

"I prefer Mrs. Vi." She blinked rapidly and then let him help her to her feet as an ambulance and another policeman came. They took Preston into the back, accompanied by one of the police officers, and then another one approached. "Or even Vi."

"Here now," he said, staring at Violet as though she were a criminal, "what happened?"

"Back off, Jenkins," the local bobby said. "This is Jack Wakefield's wife and that blackguard hunted her, broke into the house, shot a guard, the butler, and tried to kidnap Mrs. Wakefield."

Jenkins backed off, and then Jack was there and the chill that had descended into her bones started to dissipate.

~

"HE'S GOING TO HANG," Jack said flatly. "Not even for what happened to Simone but for killing Smith's man."

"Is Hargreaves really all right?" Vi demanded. "He took care of me even though he was shot."

"He's being cooed over by Kate and I believe Ham told the nurses that if Hargreaves wanted for anything at all, he'd ensure they'd all discover the wrong side of a prison cell." Victor brushed Vi's hair back. "You weren't supposed to be so slow."

"You weren't supposed to leave if he wasn't following," Vi shot back.

"He slipped us and by the time we realized and rushed back, you'd already taken care of business," Jack told her. He clenched her good hand too hard, and she didn't complain in the least because it anchored her.

"What about Smith's man?" Vi asked.

Jack paused and then shook his head once.

Vi gasped and then whispered, "Does Smith know his family? Is there something we can do?" Violet was sick that the man had been killed protecting her. That they'd all been at risk because of her.

"Smith said he didn't have family. Not that not having a family makes what happened to him all right, but at least others aren't suffering as well."

Vi shivered. "What was his name?"

Jack paused, but Victor spoke up.

"He went by Will Gode. He was one of Smith's collection of rogues. He had blonde hair, enjoyed company with a lady of the night named Esmerelda, he preferred beer to harder liquors, mocked anyone for drinking wine, and had a dog named Spot. He'll shortly be joining our house as long as there isn't somewhere else better suited for the old boy. Smith said Gode was as mean as a snake but reliable. And that his work, if not his personality, would be missed."

Vi was somehow unsurprised and also didn't quite believe it. There was a heart behind Smith's pragmatism and angel face.

Jack studied her. "You needed to know his name, didn't you?"

"Someone should remember him."

"I think we all will at that."

Violet was silent for a moment, committing the man to memory. She suspected Jack and Victor were doing the same.

"And Jude Brown?" she finally asked.

"Beaten within an inch of his life," Jack admitted, "when he tried to stop Preston. Heather found him. He wouldn't let her get him help, but he ran for the local bobby who has the beat closest to the park."

Vi's eyes welled with tears for a moment, and then she dabbed them away as she said, "I had just been thinking I thought it was him."

"He really is a fan," Victor told her. "I visited him while you were getting stitched up and he told me he recognized how you were running from his cousin from our books. He's an odd man, but he's a friend for life."

"If he's that big of a fan, you should work him into our book," Violet said, sitting up as more people entered the small hospital room. Soon her hospital bed was ringed with more friends than any one person deserved. She teared up at their smiling faces, her gaze landing on Hargreaves and nodding at him.

After greetings and careful embraces, Vi shooed everyone

but Rita and Lila away so they could help her change. She heard Hargreaves say he would go for the auto, but he was stopped by Ham who went instead, although Hargreaves followed along. A moment later, Denny said he'd go check on Jude Brown, and then she heard her husband and her twin whispering low.

When she was dressed again, she was wearing one of her favorite blush pink dresses, accented by a bandage on her arm, and a sling to hold her arm against her body. It clashed terribly, she thought, and she was far too pale to pull off anything other than the victim of something awful. It wasn't a look she wanted to keep.

"You look fabulous," Lila lied.

"I want red lipstick at least," Vi announced. "And a cloche to hide the mess of my hair."

Rita laughed and stepped in, opening her handbag. When Vi had decided they'd done what could be done, she wrapped in her furs because she loved them and then she swept back the curtain, grinning at Jack and Victor. Victor scooped Vi into his arms before Jack could get her first.

"Yet again, you're the one who saves us all," Victor told her. "Don't you remember that it's my job to protect you? Has been since the day you were born, and here you go showing me up again."

Vi didn't bother to answer. She was too busy sympathy crying at the shine in his eyes.

He set her gently down and kissed her on the forehead. "I'll squeeze the life out of you when you aren't hurting."

Vi winked at him and then looked at the doctor. "Am I free?"

"Your arm will heal and all signs of shock are gone.

Normally, I'd make you stay and keep an eye on you, but your husband has bribed one of my nurses to do just that."

Vi smiled up at Jack and then she said, "Do you hear that?"

He stared at her, concern filling his gaze. There was nothing but the sound of nurses working and the murmuring of patients.

She laughed. "That's what freedom sounds like. He's out of our lives."

Jack's dark, furious gaze told her that Preston Bates would soon be out of life in general, but Jack was too controlled to gloat aloud. "Paris, then? I believe I have a promise to keep."

"Shall we just get in the auto and drive away?" Vi asked. "No clothes, no bags, nothing?"

"Romantic getaways should be spontaneous," Jack agreed. "We've money enough to find something that will do while we're there."

"No," the doctor cut in. "A nurse needs to keep an eye on her for at least 48 hours. Then if you want to escape to Paris, you may."

Vi gasped, "He's a ruiner of fun." Her stage whisper had her friends laughing.

Vi cleared her throat, trying to hide the giddiness and knowing she failed. She could only hope that the giddiness that was hitting her disguised the horror that was embedded in the back of her mind, her stomach, and along her spine. She thought she might have succeeded with all but Victor and Jack, who watched her like hawks.

"Fine, home," Violet said, nodding at the doctor. "We'll obey. But then Durham, Paris, somewhere warm, and the country house."

"I'm in for the warm," Victor said. "Now that Kate is only sicking up in the morning, we're feeling the haunting melody of freedom ourselves."

"As long as you're back in June," Rita said idly. "For our big day. Wedding bells and all that."

Everyone paused and the cheer that filled the air was enough to help shake away the horror. If Vi was very lucky, she might even escape nightmares. But even with her dreams, she'd wake to the arms of the man who loved her, the security of friends who would do anything for her, and the knowledge that she was safe again.

The END

Hullo friends! I am so grateful you dove in and read the latest Vi book. If you wouldn't mind, I would be so grateful for a review.

THE SEQUEL to this book is available now.

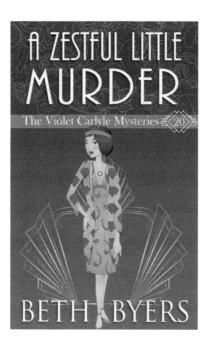

May 1926

Violet and Jack have gone to the country with their friends. They've decided to dive into the joys of a country life for the summer. Swimming, fishing with a large dose of napping.

While they're enjoying the spring, Vi gets pulled into helping to plan and pull off a May Day celebration. She anticipates organizing games and possibly judging scones or flower bouquets. What she doesn't envision is to stumble over a body and be pulled into the most unexpected of murder investigations.

Order Your Copy Here.

My newest series is now available. Keep on flipping for a sneak peak.

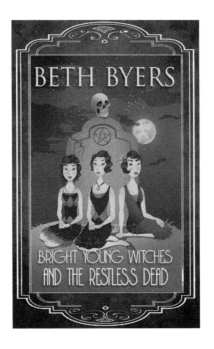

April 1922

When the Ku Klux Klan appears at the door of the Wode sisters, they decide it's time to visit the ancestral home in England.

With squabbling between the sisters, it takes them too long to realize that their new friend is being haunted. Now they'll have to set aside their fight, discover just why their friend is being haunted, and what they're going to do about it. Will they rid their friend of the ghost and out themselves as witches? Or will they look away?

Join the Wodes as they rise up and embrace just who and what they are in this newest historical mystery adventure.

Order Your Copy Here or keep on scrolling for the first chapter.

SNEAK PEEK OF BRIGHT YOUNG WITCHES & THE RESTLESS DEAD

APRIL 1922. WASHINGTON D.C. USA

ARIADNE EUDORA WISTERIA WODE

"Give me some of the good stuff," the man said, nudging a waiting girl aside. He was wearing a pinstriped evening suit with his hair pomaded back. Given the large ring on his pinky and the gold on his watch chain, Ariadne assumed he was quite wealthy or quite powerful or both. The large cigar hanging from his mouth suggested both.

Ariadne had been just behind him when he went shoving people about and she caught the girl he'd sent stumbling off her bar stool. The height of the girl's heels didn't help, but the man hadn't even noticed he'd knocked the woman down. The girl shot him a nasty, unnoticed look and then turned to Ariadne with a glance that said, *Can you believe this dirty bloke?*

"We're out," the barman said. "Want a Coke?"

The shelves behind him were nearly empty of bottles, unlike the bar itself, which was full. Ariadne sighed. The speakeasy never ordered enough, always ran low, and then the boss took it out on her. He needed either more suppliers, to quit under-ordering, or to open a little less often. Some of the fellows in the bar were reeling drunk and could have been cut off before they'd reached that state. Sloppy drunks put everyone at risk of getting pinched.

"Give me what the management is drinking," the man growled. "I know you got the good stuff, and I don't want any of this second-rate swill that'll leave me blind or dead."

"Our delivery of the good stuff is late," the barman said flatly. Whoever this shove-y man was, the barman was unimpressed. "No one's drinking much until that comes along. Not even the boss man."

Ariadne met the barman's gaze, and he jerked his head to the back. There was a triggerman guarding the door, and the man didn't move when Ariadne approached. His dark eyes fixed on hers, and there was threat in his stony expression.

Here we go again, Ariadne thought, ignoring his look and sliding past him without a flicker of a lash. Posturing was such a gent's move. She had too much to do for this nonsense. When she felt someone watching her, she glanced back and caught the gaze of a bloke with dark, sharp eyes and slicked back hair, with a hefty drink in front of him. He was, she thought, almost certainly a copper. Hopefully he was dirty. Otherwise, they'd all be hauled away with time in the slammer. The goons anyway. The shadows liked Ariadne.

Either way, she wished she was a little less memorable in the drop-waisted, shimmery dress that showed off far more of her chest than she'd prefer. She dressed with the intent to blend in with the other dames. Better to be seen as an easy moll than what she was—a lady-legger. Or, more accurately, a booze-making witch.

"It's about time," Blind Bobby growled as Ariadne appeared. "Do you have it? I don't pay full price for late goods. You're costing me a pile of lettuce, girl."

"They had checkpoints on the way in. I had to think quick and step even more quickly. You're lucky I'm here at all, and you'll be paying me the full amount or I'll take a walk down to the next juice joint. Easy peasy." She snapped her fingers. It was always better not to be too challenging, but sometimes she couldn't help herself.

Blind Bobby put his gun on the table and leaned back. "Maybe I'll just take the booze and pay you nothing, little girl."

"Did you find someone else who makes gin that won't blind you and can age wine and whisky with magic—because I don't think you have found anyone like me."

"I'll pay you eighty percent." He sniffed and growled, "From here on."

His dark, beady eyes fixed on her, and he leaned in, strong jaw gritted. He intended to scare her, but Ariadne was only irritated. She felt as though every time she interacted with this grunting beast, he thought he could just tower over her face and she'd crumple. Ariadne laughed, a trilling thing that didn't sound amused but conveyed her message.

Blind Billy nudged his gun once again, and Ariadne scowled at him, dropping all pretense of amusement. She crossed her arms over her chest and lifted a challenging brow instead. "Do you really want to put a *bean* shooter up against magic?"

"Do you really want to put you and your little sister

against my boys? There's even smaller witch brats in that town of yours. What's it called? Nighton? Bring her in." The last was said to one of the apes standing about grasping their guns trying to look intimidating.

There was a sound at the tunnel door and several men poured through with Ariadne's sister, Echo. She struggled in the grasp of...Ariadne's head cocked and gaze narrowed.

Lindsey Noel. She scowled at him. He was the shining son of Nighton and the fellow intent on finding his way into Ariadne's sister Circe's knickers.

"Well, if it isn't Lindsey Noel. Are you joining in on threatening my sisters? *All* of my sisters?"

Lindsey blushed, but his voice was mean. "I know where you live." His fingers dug into Echo's bicep.

"And I know where you live." Ariadne glanced at Echo, who seemed fine despite the white circles under Lindsey's pressing fingers. "Why'd you let them take you?"

"I wanted to see what Lindsey was up to. Sooner or later, Circe will see he's milquetoast playing at being a leading man. She believes that front he puts up, but the mannered handsome puppy will fade into what he really is—another arrogant rube with a rich daddy. It'll go easier if it's me telling her what he did, and after all—he put his hands on me."

Easier, Ariadne translated, than if Ari were the one who told Circe her lover put them all at risk with his playing at being a bad boy.

The idiot Lindsey let go of Echo, but it was too late. The smirk she shot him was enough to have him wondering, would he lose Circe over this? The unfortunate answer was that Ariadne could only wish.

The other men glanced at each other, smirking, when

Blind Billy grunted, "No one cares about your hick problems." He gestured and the goons lining the wall leveled their guns at Ariadne.

She sighed. "Until I get paid, you won't be able to open the bottles at the delivery point. Try as you might."

Blind Bobby laughed meanly and Ariadne yawned. He shoved the table back, grabbing his gun as he did, and shoved it into Ariadne's face, pressing it hard against her forehead.

"Careful," she said quietly, "guns do malfunction so easily."

"Open the whiskey, Petey," Blind Billy ordered.

Ariadne rolled her eyes and telepathically told her sister, *Draw your magic.* Ariadne opened her mind and senses to her own magic. She'd originally approached Blind Billy once prohibition went into effect because the church basement where the speakeasy was housed was a place of power. Her magic, always strong, thrummed through her with a vengeance here. Echo's must be a tsunami of power given the dead that even Ariadne could sense.

The ghosts are restless, Echo sent.

Of course they are, it's a desecrated church. How did Noel know about us?

Echo's mental snort seemed to ricochet about Ariadne's head and they both knew the answer: Circe. Soft, trusting, blind-with-love Circe. Lindsey Noel wasn't surprised in the least by their magic. Their sister hated keeping what they were from her 'sweet' Lindsey. She must have talked, and he'd gathered a full confession, given his presence.

Foolish girl.

The grunting of his man trying to open the bottle caught her attention. The goon was yanking at the stopper in the whiskey bottle, desperate to open it. He finally brought out a large knife, but it bounded off of the glass as though it were stone instead of a little bit of cork and glass. Finally he looked up at Blind Billy and shook his head.

Blind Billy pulled the gun back enough just to shove it back against her head again. "That's gonna leave a bruise." His laugh was ugly and he glanced at his men until they were snorting with unbelievable laughter as well.

"Balm of Gilead is an easy enough potion to make for someone like me," Ariadne told him, drawing her magic so deeply that her bobbed hair was slowly starting to rise around her face. "The bruise will be gone in minutes. I carry it in my handbag."

"What about the hole my bullet leaves?" He cocked his gun and then, to her horror, swung his arm wide, aiming at Echo. "Will it cure that?"

"Fool," Ariadne said, finished with this nonsense. She dropped to her knees, covering her head when the gun misfired, and magic rushed into Ariadne as the place of power energized her and she sent the rest of the guns into either misfiring or not firing at all.

With Echo there, ghosts were caught in the energy in the church and within the sisters. The ghosts went mad, merging into a tornado of shadows that sent Blind Billy's goons into shrieking like little girls. Point of fact, Ariadne thought as she started to crawl away from Blind Billy, her little sisters wouldn't have whined like these boys.

A moment later, the copper from earlier rushed the door. Ariadne dropped her magic immediately so it seemed that the screaming goons had gone crazy. On her knees, with forced tears, she looked like a victim as she reached for the copper. She screamed to draw his attention to her from Echo. "Help! Help me, please!"

Police swarmed the room, and Ariadne was yanked to her feet by the first copper to reach her. He glanced her over, muttered, "Fool doll," and shoved her behind him.

She shivered and whimpered and thanked the whole of the group repetitively with big crocodile tears, backing towards the wall. Her dress, her mussed makeup, and her tears were enough for the blokes to not realize she was one of the criminals. Just another doll caught up with the wrong man. She waited until they were all looking the other way, wrestling the goons down, and she slid into the shadows, pulling them around her.

The coppers didn't know about the escape tunnel where Echo had already disappeared, followed by Lindsey Noel. Echo had sealed it against any but Ariadne, so the fuzz were gathering up the men who couldn't use their tunnel while she slipped through, cloaked in darkness and magic.

Using the athamé in her handbag, Ariadne carved a rune of the door to keep it locked. She ignored the skittering of rats and the cool touch of the dead as she hurried down the tunnel.

"Go back to sleep," she murmured to the dead, hoping they'd comply. Otherwise the boys who worked for Blind Billy would find themselves chilled in body and spirit.

The old church had a crypt underneath, so it was better not to look into the dark entrances of side rooms if you wanted to avoid looking at the remnants of the living. The tunnels went from the crypt to beyond the graveyard behind the church, following beneath the road. Blind Billy's men had extended the tunnels even farther. With that kind of work ethic, what might those goons have been capable of if they bothered working for good?

Ariadne mocked herself—knowing she was a criminal too

—and moved quickly through the tunnels. There were exits for a good mile down the tunnel road if you knew where to look and what to look for.

The vast majority of Ariadne's booze delivery was still in the auto garage where one of the exits from the tunnels led. The bottles were loaded on the back of her truck. Echo already had their truck running and was just loading the last of the whiskey bottles that had been previously unloaded. Any speakeasy could make gin in their bathtub. Magically aged liqueurs, wines, and whiskey required a witch, a different country, or a very expensive operation that risked prison time. Ariadne sealed the tunnel behind her with the same rune she'd used before. Someone would have to find the runes she'd used and destroy them before the exit would open. Otherwise it would take hours for the spell to fade.

She looked away from her spell and eyed her sister. Echo looked a little mussed but none the worse for wear. "Anyone left here?"

"Just Timmy," Echo grunted as she grabbed the bag of their clothes from behind the truck's seat. "Poor boy. My spell got him hard in the gut when he tried to dodge. He'll have sore ribs if Blind Billy doesn't kill him for losing us and the booze."

"Did Lindsey get out?" Ariadne asked as she shimmied out of her evening gown. Echo tossed Ariadne a wool skirt and blouse, and they stripped down in the auto garage, changing from party clothes to one step away from an initiate for a nunnery.

"He got out when I did, but he was bright enough not to follow me here. We need to consider a change of employment. If things had gone differently, Circe would be raising Medea and Cassiopeia. I love Circe, but..."

Ariadne winced. It was true. If there had been more coppers or if the fellows were a little more trigger happy, they'd have been in trouble. With enough guns blazing, even witches wouldn't have survived.

Ariadne told Echo, "Aunt Beatrix said she was interested in taking over. She has more people. That...that...flimflam that just happened to us wouldn't have happened to her. Not with her sons. Jasper and Gerard with those broad shoulders and thick jaws? Let alone their magic? They won't get the same garbage we're getting."

"We'll still get our cut too," Echo reminded Ariadne with a telling glance. "Beatrix promised it when she wanted to take on the work. You engineered the spells for aging the booze like we do, and Beatrix knows it. We have to be careful, Ariadne—at least until Medea and Cassiopeia are older. They're too little to lose you too."

It wasn't Echo's words that convinced Ariadne. It was the memory of the gun being swung her sister's way. If Echo hadn't been prepared for someone to turn their gun on her, if her magic hadn't been inclined towards the dead, if they'd been firing guns haphazardly, if the sisters had been a little less lucky, Ariadne might have lost her sister. No amount of dough was worth that.

Order Your Copy Here.

ALSO BY BETH BYERS

The Violet Carlyle Historical Mysteries

Murder & the Heir

Murder at Kennington House

Murder at the Folly

A Merry Little Murder

New Year's Madness: A Short Story Anthology

Valentine's Madness: A Short Story Anthology

Murder Among the Roses

Murder in the Shallows

Gin & Murder

Obsidian Murder

Murder at the Ladies Club

Weddings Vows & Murder

A Jazzy Little Murder

Murder by Chocolate

A Friendly Little Murder

Murder by the Sea

Murder On All Hallows

Murder in the Shadows

A Jolly Little Murder

Hijinks & Murder

Love & Murder

A Zestful Little Murder

A Murder Most Odd

Nearly A Murder

The Poison Ink Mysteries

Death By the Book

Death Witnessed

Death by Blackmail

Death Misconstrued

Deathly Ever After

Death in the Mirror

A Merry Little Death

Death Between the Pages

The Hettie & Ro Adventures

co-written with Bettie Jane

Philanderers Gone

Adventurer Gone

Holiday Gone

Aeronaut Gone

The Second Chance Diner Mysteries

Spaghetti, Meatballs, & Murder

Cookies & Catastrophe

Poison & Pie

Double Mocha Murder

Printed in Great Britain
by Amazon

18150273R00107